# FATHER, LIKE SON?

12 stories about
boys and their dads

EDITED BY

# TONY BRADMAN

KINGFISHER

For my dad... and my son. TB

KINGFISHER
An imprint of Kingfisher Publications Plc
New Penderel House, 283-288 High Holborn
London WC1V 7HZ
www.kingfisherpub.com

First published by Kingfisher 2006
2 4 6 8 10 9 7 5 3 1

ISBN-13: 978 0 7534 1119 3
ISBN-10: 0 7534 1111 9

Printed in India
1TR/1205/THOM/SCHOY/70STORA/C

# Contents

# Introduction

I've always been deeply fascinated by stories about fathers and sons. I could say that's because it's a very important subject, but the truth is that it's probably because I don't feel I ever really knew my own dad.

My parents got divorced when I was seven, and my dad's job took him abroad a lot. So there were large stretches of my childhood when I hardly saw him at all. Although strangely enough, the less I saw of him, the larger he seemed to loom in my mind. I thought about him all the time. I wondered where he was and what he was doing. I loved getting postcards from the exotic places his job took him to, and read them over and over again. I longed for him to come home, for him simply to be here.

I also remember being very envious of friends whose parents weren't divorced, boys with dads who gave them advice and showed them how to fix things and played football with them, or better still, came to watch them play for school teams. That's what I wanted – a dad to tell me what to do, and to give me his approval when I did something well.

Most of my friends took their fathers for granted, and by the time I was a teenager I realized a real flesh and blood dad is rather more complicated than an ideal father in your head. I was seeing my dad regularly by then, and although he gave me a lot of the approval I'd been looking for, we also had plenty of disagreements. He didn't like my long hair and jeans. I didn't like his politics. And we were both embarrassed by each other.

The years passed. I grew up, got married, became a dad myself, to two beautiful daughters. Things didn't go so well for my dad. His business went bust, and like many men in that position he felt bitterly disappointed with the way his life had turned out. After all, aren't men supposed to be ambitious and strive for success? To be good providers for their families? Still, it was a time when at least we were talking more, and for a while I thought there was a chance I might even get to know him a little better.

But it wasn't to be. My dad had been quite ill for several years, and suddenly he was absent again, only now there was no chance that he would come back. His death came as a huge shock, partly because my own writing career was starting to take off and I wanted him to see I was doing well. But also because a few months later our third child was born – a son.

It almost seemed spookily strange it should turn out that way.

So I found myself wondering what kind of father I should be to my son Thomas. Certainly not an absent one. When my parents split up (in the early 1960s), divorce was pretty unusual. But by the time I became a parent it was a lot more common, and many children were growing up without fathers around. I didn't want that to happen to my kids.

But should I be Dad the Disciplinarian, the stern father who lays down the law and hands out punishment when it's broken? Or should I be Dad the Teacher, the guy who knows everything and shows his son how the world works? Or should I just be Dad the Friend, a playful companion with a car and a credit card? But of course, what I soon learned was that being a dad meant I had to be all of those things, and a lot more besides.

Sons want a dad they can look up to and respect, a dad who gives them approval and love. But sons also want a dad they can react to, even rebel against. As sons, some of us discover that we want to grow up to be like our dads, and some of us are absolutely terrified in case that happens. Sons worry they might be a disappointment to their dads. Dads worry they're letting their sons down. Many of us feel all of those things, so it's no wonder that we men sometimes find it hard to express our emotions.

But one emotion I can express is a delight in the stories you're about to read. It's been fascinating to see how the experiences of writers from Britain, the US and Australia have been similar to mine. Like father, like son, indeed. In these pages you'll find every kind of dad, and every kind of son too, and discover how they get on with each other. Or don't, as the case may be. I think my dad would be proud of me for putting together such a terrific book, and that my own son will enjoy reading it.

I'm sure you will too.

*Tony Bradman*

# The Wordwatcher

## Joseph Wallace

"Look!" Dad says. "Approaching the road verge! A scrub jay!"

Right then, our car coughs (like someone swallowing wrong), gurgles (like a baby crying), groans (like my brother does when I make a joke)… and dies.

Dad pulls to the side of the road just in time. I look around. Yep, we're halfway between Nowhere and Nowhere Else, Arizona. There are no other cars in sight, nothing but grey bushes and cactuses and the black, empty road in both directions as far as I can see. The only things moving under the hot afternoon sun are the mirages, which look like dancing pools of water on the road but which disappear when you get close to them. If your car is still moving.

I can hear the dead engine popping and a bird squawking. For all I know, it's the scrub jay.

"Uh-oh," Dad says. "It appears that our trusty steed has succumbed to the inevitable effect of the inability of the internal-combustion engine to function indefinitely on the merest wisps of sublimated distilled petroleum."

Understand that? Well, I do. All that talk of trusty steeds and sublimated petroleum – it's the way you'd say, "This car's been running on fumes, and now it's out of gas."

That is, it's the way you'd say it if you were a normal person, and not Mr Strange.

I mean, *Dr* Strange.

Dad's a doctor, or, as he calls it, a "physician". Whenever he stubs his toe or bangs his head (and, since he's really tall and skinny and has these long legs, this happens often), he says, "Physician, heal thyself!" and then laughs. No one else thinks it's funny, but he doesn't care. He just says, "Physician, amuse thyself!" and laughs some more.

He works at Memorial Hospital and in an office down at the Medical Arts Building in our town in Westchester County, which is just outside New York City. He's a rheumatologist, which means a doctor who treats people who have arthritis. Arthritis is when your joints ache and you have to take pills to feel better.

Once when I was little I heard him call himself a "sawbones", which I guess is another way of saying doctor. But I heard it as "sore bones", and that's still how I think of what he does – he treats people who have sore bones.

Dad's not the kind of doctor who spends a lot of time running down corridors or yelling orders in the emergency room, like doctors do on TV. In fact, I think a rheumatologist isn't really much of a doctor at all. Maybe that's why he calls himself a "physician", because it makes him sound more important than he really is.

I can't believe it. "We're out of gas?"

"I think so," Dad says, tapping the little dial on the dashboard, as if that's going to help.

"How could it happen?"

"We were betrayed by the fuel gauge," he says, sounding sad.

"Betrayed?" I ask. "How? Did it say the tank was full?"

"No, it reported that the tank was empty," he tells me.

I look at him.

"When the gauge registers *Empty*," he says, "I've always been of the belief that the gasoline tank will harbour at least another gallon of fuel. More than sufficient to carry us to the next establishment where gasoline is offered for sale."

I close my eyes. It figures he'd do this to us. I mean, this trip was supposed to be for *me*. It was *my* thirteenth birthday two months ago, *my* bar mitzvah last month, *my* present. A trip with just Dad, without my brother and sister. Just the two of us.

And here we are, sitting in a dead car on an empty road miles from anywhere.

Couldn't he do things like everyone else for just one week?

"What are we going to do now?" I ask. My voice sounds a little babyish in my ears, which I hate. But I'm wondering if we're going to be stuck here for hours... maybe overnight... before someone finds us, and though I don't want to admit it, the idea is scary.

Dad has his cell phone out, the silly cheap one he got at 7-Eleven. "It's a phone, Jack," he said when I begged him to get a flip phone with a video camera, net access, games, text messaging, and downloadable wallpaper. "Why should I surrender five times as much hard-earned remuneration so my telephone can do a mediocre – or even wretched – imitation of what a camera, a computer, a cable connection and an interior decorator can accomplish far more ably?"

An interior decorator? Oh, I get it: "Wallpaper".

Dad is staring down at the teeny screen on his dumb little phone. "It appears to be roaming," he says, and then starts singing, "Roam, roam on the range, where the microchips and satellites play..."

Then he frowns and slips the phone back in his pocket. "No service," he says.

*Of course there's no service!* I want to yell at him.

*We're in Nowhere, Arizona! In fact, we haven't even made it to Nowhere yet!*

But instead I just say again, "What are we going to do?"

Dad smiles at me. There's already sweat shining on his bald head, but he seems totally cheerful.

"It's a magnificent day for an expedition," he says, waving out towards the empty road with its dancing mirages. "Shall we perambulate?"

My Dad is really smart. Everyone knows that. He's so smart that half the time you need a dictionary to understand what he's saying.

I'm serious. He'll step outside after dinner, take a deep breath, smile, and say, "Ahh, the gloaming!"

Do you know what "gloaming" means? I didn't either, until I looked it up.

It means "evening".

Dad is so smart that he was only sixteen when he went off to college somewhere down South, and only nineteen when he graduated. He had the third best average of anyone in his college class, even though everyone else was two or three years older than he was. Like I said: smart.

Unfortunately, being smart doesn't mean that you have a clue.

"During the rainy season, torrential downpours in distant mountains sometimes create great flash floods here. It's an awe-inspiring display of nature's fury," Dad says, pointing at a dry, dusty gully. It's as hot and dry as the inside of a pizza oven.

I look at him through the sweat pouring down my forehead into my eyes. It stings, like when you open your eyes underwater in a swimming pool or the ocean. But at least underwater it's cool, and wet.

"Though I believe that in the rainy season," Dad says, "you don't run such a sobering risk of encountering venomous serpents."

I look at him. "Venomous serpents?" I ask. "You mean… like rattlesnakes?"

Already I can hear the deadly tick-tick-tick sound in my ears, and every stick along the side of the road seems about to raise a fanged face at me.

"Yes, but I believe most will not venture out until dusk, when the worst of the heat has abated." Suddenly his gaze moves to above my head, and his eyes widen. "Look," he says.

I look up, almost expecting to see a flying rattler. But it's only a flock of small birds with pointy wings darting and swooping over the road. There must be a hundred of them.

"Ahh, violet-green swallows," Dad tells me. "Did you know each one consumes thousands of flying arthropods *every day*?"

"No," I say. Mostly what I know right now is that

there's sweat pouring down my neck, my arms, my legs. I think the road is melting, because it seems to be holding onto the bottoms of my sneakers each time I lift a foot. Everything smells like tar.

"It's true," Dad says. "Swallows have among the finest eyesight and quickest reflexes of any creature on earth."

Dad, on the other hand, wears glasses whose lenses are as thick as the safety windows in our school. He can't see three feet without them. If he was a violet-green swallow, he'd be doomed. He'd starve to death trying to catch one flying bug, forget thousands.

Then again, if he was a swallow, he might not even last long enough to starve to death. He'd fly headfirst into a tree while he was using big words in swallowese to drive his swallow kids crazy.

Dad's still looking up at the birds, which are almost over our heads now. Then he says, "Imagine what it would be like to be a gnat and see that vast avian assemblage approaching!" He flaps his arms, as if desperately trying to escape the deadly horde. "Oh, no!" he cries, flapping. "We're doomed!"

A minute ago, I was hoping a car would pull up and give us a ride. But now I'm glad we're alone.

A lot of doctors have to work on weekends, but not Dad. I guess his patients with arthritis don't really need him until Monday. I should be happy about that, but I have to say, sometimes I wish he was around less.

He doesn't dress like any of the other fathers in the neighbourhood do on their days off. Dad gets up on Saturday mornings and puts on the kind of clothes most other men wear to work. I mean, like these neat blue pants and a shirt you have to button up the front, with a collar and everything. And a sports jacket. And black shoes.

Sometimes he even wears a tie. On the weekend!

Other fathers play catch with their kids. Dad has an old baseball glove, which he first got back like in 1970, but he doesn't use it much, not these days. He used to go out and play catch with me every once in a while, but it never lasted long. Pretty soon he'd be making faces and rubbing the back of his shoulder, and that would be that.

"I've got burstitis," he told me. Or at least that's what I thought he said, and at first I thought he meant that something had burst inside his shoulder. I got this visual of tons of stuff like red chilli bubbling around in there, and when he said he had to stop throwing the ball, I didn't argue.

But then I looked up the word, and found it was really spelled "bursitis". And you know what it basically was? Sore bones.

Figures.

"Do you see that bird?" Dad asks.

*Another bird?* I think, though I don't say anything. I have so much sweat in my eyes that I can barely see where he's pointing, but then I get a look at a small grey-and-black bird perched on top of a thornbush beside the road. It's staring at us with an eye like a shining black button.

"That," Dad says, in a voice that's so proud and happy it's as if he built the bird himself, "is a loggerhead shrike."

"Uh-huh," I say.

"Shrikes," he goes on, leading us a little closer, "are, gram for gram, perhaps the most ferocious carnivorous predators on earth. They confront creatures twice their size, with only their beaks as weapons. But what a beak!"

The shrike's beak is sharp and hooked. Now that we're close enough to see it clearly, it does actually look pretty fierce.

"And after it has disposed of a sparrow or a mouse, you know what it does next?"

"What?" I say, though I know he's going to tell me anyway.

"It eats as much as it feels like, and then impales the rest on a nearby thorn, or on a piece of barbed wire, if one is present."

I think about this. The shrike lifts its head, as if it's been listening too and likes what Dad said.

"You mean," I say, "if we look closely at this bush, we might see a mouse with a thorn through it?"

Dad nods. "Very likely."

"Ewwww," I say.

"Yes," Dad agrees. "The magnificent panoply of nature, filled with wonders grisly enough to banish the latest horror movie from the silver screen in shame."

Why can't he just say, "Ewwww"?

In case you haven't figured it out yet, what Dad loves the most is birds. No, that's not true – it's every living thing he loves. "The panoply of nature" – I've heard him use that phrase before.

Some of the other fathers on our street like to work in their gardens. But Dad doesn't care to. You can tell because our bushes look like giant wigs, and our flowers lie down on the ground instead of standing up in rows. If Mom didn't spend some time keeping it under control, we'd be living in a jungle.

The problem with gardens, Dad says, is that they're all too much the same. What he loves are the surprises, the unexpected. "Every yard is a veritable universe," he says, "and we're the astronauts exploring uncharted new worlds."

Which means that while Mr Hester across the street is planting an azalea bush, Dad is in our yard turning over rocks. Or studying something on a leaf through a magnifying glass. Or climbing one of the pine trees we have in the back. Or just standing there in the middle of the lawn, staring up at the sky.

When I was little, Dad and I would go on "safaris" through the neighbourhood, and we never knew what we might find: a praying mantis swaying on a branch, a slithery salamander under a log, baby cardinals in their nest. It was fun. I could see what Dad meant when he said we were like explorers, and our street was the African plains or the Amazon jungle.

He'd even wear this funny hat he called a "pith helmet" that he said was designed for safaris.

But then my friends started asking me why my father was so weird. "Safaris?" they'd say. "He should go on safari to the loony bin."

After that, when Dad suggested we go out exploring, I started saying no. I never told him why, and after a while he stopped asking.

Until now. This trip to Arizona was like a big safari, and Dad had been looking forwards to it for months. We started in Tucson, where he had a medical conference, which is a kind of vacation for doctors. He was getting some award. For three days, while he went to lectures and lunches, I wandered around the hotel, swam in the pool and got smiled at by a bunch of people I didn't know.

Once, an old lady grabbed my arm and said into my ear, "Do you know how wonderful a doctor your father is?"

I didn't say anything to that. But I was thinking: how wonderful can you be if you just treat sore bones?

After the conference, we left Tucson. "Destination: Chiricahuas!" Dad said, and explained that the Chiricahuas were part of a mountain range, which he called the "Sky Islands".

The Sky Islands were filled with birds Dad had never seen before. "It's an avian extravaganza!" he said. "Painted redstarts are summer residents there, and beryline hummingbirds are occasional visitors. You can even find elegant trogons!"

For a minute I thought he said "dragons".

But trogons or dragons, it didn't matter, because before we got halfway there we ran out of gas. Walking along the hot roadside, I didn't think we'd ever reach the Chiricahuas. If they'd been real islands, instead of sky ones, we would already have drowned.

"I think I see a gas station," I say.

It's hard to tell. Though the sun isn't quite as hot as it was earlier, the heat waves and mirages still make the buildings down the road seem like they're shaking back and forth. But I think I can see gas pumps and a little store where they'll have snacks and drinks. I'm getting pretty hungry and thirsty.

"I do believe you're right," Dad says. "Petroleum ho!"

We walk a little faster. Then Dad frowns and rubs a

droplet of sweat off the tip of his nose. "I hope they will be able to provide us with a transportation container."

I look at him. "A what?"

"A transportation container."

I try to figure out what he means. "You mean a can to fill up with gas?" I ask him. "Or a car to bring us and the gas back to *our* car?"

Dad blinks, then gives me a big smile. "Both!" he says. "*Two* transportation containers!"

A moment later, he's not smiling any more. "Jack," he says, and there's something in his voice that makes me feel like my heart is falling into my stomach. "Jack," he says again, "can you tell what's going on down here?"

I look where he's pointing: towards the gas station, which isn't very far away now. Squinting my eyes, I look as hard as I can.

"There's a bunch of people standing around," I say. Then, "I think someone's lying on the ground."

Without another word, Dad starts to run. He has the funniest way of running, probably because he's never done much of it. He's all legs flying this way, arms that way. Usually I'd look around to make sure no one was watching, but my heart's still in my stomach.

He looks weird, but I never noticed before how fast he can run when he wants to.

I chase after him. I can see now that I was right.

There's someone lying on the ground outside a blue SUV at one of the pumps. A man in jeans and a black Arizona Diamondbacks T-shirt, his big round stomach pushing against the shirt. He's flat on his back, his eyes are closed and his face is a shade of grey I've never seen on a person before.

Two people are squatting next to him, and about ten more are standing around. A couple of them look like they're crying. But nobody really seems to be doing anything.

I think the man with the grey face might be dead.

My father marches right into the middle of the crowd. "I'm a physician," he says. "Please give me room."

He's panting, but his voice is strong and loud, and everyone seems to understand that "physician" means doctor.

They clear space for him, and right away he's down on his knees. He puts his hand against the man's neck. Then he pushes the T-shirt up to show the man's chest and belly, which are the colour of white paper.

He looks up. "Ambulance?"

"On its way," someone says. "But it's gonna take ten, fifteen minutes to get here."

Without another word, my father leans over. His mouth opens, and then it looks like he's kissing the man. Even though I know what he's really doing –

breathing air into the man's lungs – I look away.

When I look back, my father's hands are on the man's chest, pushing down. It's a rhythm: push push push, like fifteen times, and then breathe breathe twice. Push push push breathe breathe.

I don't know how long he keeps this up, but it feels like hours. Days. A whole life. And all that time, my father never says a word. Just push push push breathe breathe.

Finally the man moves – just a little. I see his big chest heave, and one of his hands flops. Dad sits back. He's breathing hard.

And finally, *finally*, we hear the sound of the siren approaching. Just a few seconds later, the ambulance comes roaring up with its lights flashing. Two men in blue uniforms jump out and run over.

Moving like his legs hurt, my father gets to his feet. The ambulance men bend over the guy on the ground, and a minute later he's on a stretcher and inside the ambulance.

Before they leave, one of the ambulance men talks to my father. I can only hear bits and pieces of my father's answers: "Stopped?" he says. "Yes. Maybe a minute. What?" He looks at his watch. "Seventeen minutes, give or take."

The ambulance man shakes my father's hand. He looks – and I think I recognize the expression – he looks *impressed*.

And then, lights flashing and sirens wailing, they're gone.

"Dad?" I say much later.

"Yes, Jack?"

We're standing in the campground called Sunny Flats, a big grassy area surrounded by the Sky Islands of the Chiricahuas. There are a few other tents set up here and there, but no one else is around. We're both wearing our binoculars around our necks, but right now we're not looking at birds.

I've been thinking for hours, but until now I haven't felt like talking. After the ambulance left with the sick man inside, Dad stood there as everyone congratulated him. I could tell how tired he was, but he was nice, smiling and shrugging and saying that any doctor – any *physician* – would have done the same.

Then people who ran the gas station offered me anything I wanted to eat. I wasn't very hungry, but I ate a piece of pizza and some ice cream. Dad had a cup of coffee, a donut and endless glasses of water. The people told us it was all free, but Dad insisted on paying.

He did allow two of the gas station workers to drive a full gas can back to our car – one transportation container inside another. Fifteen minutes later our car was at the pump having its tank filled to the brim, while people made jokes like,

"This should last you until you head back to New York, Doc, so you won't have to bother us again."

Then we were back on the road. Dad tried asking me a few questions, but when I didn't answer he let me be quiet. He turned on the radio to some crazy country music, and the only time he spoke was to point out a golden eagle soaring like a king over the desert.

I needed time to think.

Finally, ahead of us, we saw the Chiricahuas. They really did look like islands, tall towers made of red rock outlined against the blue sky. They got bigger and bigger until we drove right into them, the road cutting through a narrow canyon with cliffs on either side.

Even standing near our tent at Sunny Flats, I feel like we're somehow inside the mountain. It's a comfortable feeling, and one that makes me finally want to talk. "Dad," I say, "was that man going to die?"

Dad takes a minute to answer. Then he says, "Yes, he'd stopped breathing. If I hadn't been there – or someone else who knew CPR – he would have died."

"You saved his life?"

Again he doesn't answer right away. "I hope so," he says finally. "When we get to a working phone, I'll call the hospital and find out. But he was breathing on his own when they took him away, which is a good sign."

A few minutes later, I say, "Dad?"

"Yes, Jack?"

"You've done that before? Saved people's lives?"

He nods.

"But I thought you just treat people with—" I almost say sore bones. "Arthritis. They don't need saving, like that man did, do they?"

"Not very often," he says. "But when you're a physician, you promise to help anyone who needs helping, whether they're your patient or not. It's a promise – an oath – you make when you first become a doctor. So you'd better know what to do."

The sun has already gone behind the red cliffs. The shadows are creeping across the campground, but the air is still warm. Ten feet away, a little animal pokes its head up from a hole in the grass. Dad smiles. "Ground squirrel," he says, and raises his binoculars to look at it.

"Dad?" I ask.

"Mm-hmm?" He's still watching the squirrel.

"Dad, why do you act so—"

I'm going to say, "weird", but at the last second I decide not to. So I say, "Why do you act so silly sometimes?"

For a second he doesn't move. Then he lowers the binoculars and looks at me. My heart is thumping in my chest.

But he doesn't seem angry or sad, just like he's

thinking about what I said. Finally he says, "Because I can. Because I'm allowed to be silly when I'm with you."

He sees that I don't understand. "You know I spend all day, almost every day, with people who are very sick," he says.

"Uh-huh."

But he sees what I'm thinking. "I know you think I only treat 'sore bones', Jack," he says, "but many of my arthritis patients are in terrible pain. I can help them feel better, but sometimes it takes a long time. Years. It's serious work, and there's not much chance to be silly."

He smiles. "So I make up for it at home. Because I can."

"Okay," I say.

Again he understands my thoughts. "But it's not so easy to have a silly dad when you're thirteen, is it?" he asks.

I shrug.

"No, I know that it isn't." He holds out his hand. "I promise to try not to embarrass you any more. At least not so much. Okay?"

"Okay," I say, and we shake hands.

Some birds fly around the cliffs. Violet-green swallows, hunting for bugs.

"Dad?" I say.

"Mm-hmm?"

"Why do you talk the way you do?"

He gives me a curious look. "What way?"

"Using all those big words that no one else understands." When he doesn't say anything, I go on. "I mean, I heard you with those guys at the gas station, and you weren't talking that way with them. And you're using regular words now too, mostly. So you don't have to talk that way, do you?"

It takes him a while to answer, and I think maybe he looks a little embarrassed. "No," he tells me. Then he waggles his hands. "Well, sometimes the big words just come out. My mouth says them before my brain knows it's going to. Do you understand that?"

I do. "You mean like when I curse, even if I don't mean to?"

"Exactly. Sometimes it's like that. But mostly," now he's smiling, "mostly I just like how big words taste."

"Taste?" I say.

He nods. "And how they feel in my mouth."

I don't know what to say to this.

"Words have textures and flavours," he says, tapping a finger against his binoculars. "Some are like spaghetti strands – your lips kind of have to slurp them up." He thinks for a second. "Reprehensible and multidisciplinary, those are spaghetti words."

"Multidisciplinary," I say slowly.

"See?" He's smiling. "And other words taste rich and dark and mysterious, like really fine chocolate. Zanzibar is a chocolate word, and so are recumbent and effulgence."

I'll look those up later.

"And still others are kind of spicy," Dad says. "Felicitations! Sarsaparilla! Your mouth tingles when you say them."

"Sass…" I say.

He helps me pronounce it correctly – sass-pa-ril-la – and then says, "See? All of them are more fun to say than the drab, boring words everyone uses every day. They taste better. I mean, why say 'hi' when you can say, 'Greetings and felicitations!' Especially if you bow and sweep off your hat as you say it."

I look around, but no one is in sight. "Greetings," I say, bowing and sweeping off my pretend hat. "Felicitations!"

Dad laughs. Then he leans close to me, as if he's going to share a big secret. "Want to hear one of my favourites?" he asks. "It's just about the tastiest word I know."

"Sure," I say.

"Tsutsugamuchi," he says.

I stare at him.

He laughs. "Say it with me. Tsutsugamuchi."

"Tsu-tu…" I say.

"Tsu-tsu-ga-mu-chi," he says. "It's a disease with symptoms like arthritis. That's why I know about it. But what's important is that it's so much fun to say. Try it: tsutsugamuchi."

"Tsutsugamuchi," I say.

And he's right, it does taste good. It makes my mouth tingle.

"And it's even better if you say it loud." Dad puts his head back and hollers, "TSUTSUGAMUCHI!"

The sound echoes off the cliffs all around. The ground squirrel squeaks and disappears down its hole. If there's anyone within three miles of us, they must think the campground has been invaded by crazy people.

But suddenly I don't care. "TSUTSUG-AMUCHI!" I shout at the top of my lungs. The swallows fly away, as if they think I might be hunting *them*.

"TSUTSUGAMUCHI IN THE CHIRIC-AHUAS!" Dad and I bellow together, laughing so hard there are tears rolling down our faces.

Then a bird flies out of a distant tree towards us and lands on a branch just a few feet away, as if wondering who's making all that noise. I can tell right away that it's something we haven't seen before, with its shining green back and yellow beak and belly that's as red and round as an apple.

"Ohh," Dad says. He and I raise our binoculars at the same moment.

"The elegant trogon," he whispers. "A Sky Island specialty."

The trogon looks at us for another second, then flies away and out of sight. We watch it go.

I'm about to say, "Cool bird!" But then I stop myself. Why not?

"Bravo!" I say. "A breathtaking ornithological participant in the panoply of nature. A rainbow of avian magnificence from the top of its verdant crown to the tip of its coppery tail."

Dad's eyes are wide. "Wow," he says. "How did *those* words taste?"

"Like spaghetti," I tell him. "Like chocolate and salsa."

He shakes his head, then reaches out and puts a hand on my shoulder. "You're my son, all right," he says.

And you know what?

I'm okay with that.

# My Dad's a Punk

## SEAN TAYLOR

He's got seven earrings and red, spiked-up hair. He goes round in tartan trousers with zips all over and this leather jacket with "Bucket of Snot" written on the back. "Bucket of Snot" is the band he plays in with his mates Trevor and Biscuit.

You get used to it. When Dad still lived here with Mum and me, I'd come home from school and find the living-room windows rattling because the band was rehearsing. Their favourite song was called "It Beats Being Hit on the Head with a Rabbit". Dad moved out more than a year ago. Mum told him to go. At first, he wouldn't. He kept saying I'd need to have him around. My mum put her foot down though, and then he left. But he only moved a few streets away, to Biscuit's place.

It was a big change. Mum's a nurse and she works a lot of late shifts. So I've always spent loads of time with Dad. Biscuit's flat is a madhouse. Once, after Dad moved there, I dropped round and found the two of them had spent the whole afternoon dyeing

Trevor's dog pink. The kitchen's always full of take-away cartons, plates and empty cans. Dad sleeps on the sofa. He says he likes the place because it's close enough for me to come over whenever I want.

I'm meant to stay round with him every other weekend but I'm not really into that. There's hardly space for two people, let alone three. I prefer just paying Dad a visit when I can. He always wants me to stay and have another cup of tea. Then he plugs in his guitar and wants me to hear some new song he's writing. But I never stay long. I've got my routine to stick to.

I swim seriously. I've been going to Vale Road Swimming Club since I was six. These days I train four times a week. When Dad sees me setting the alarm for 5.45 a.m. he tells me I'm crazy. But you've got to take it seriously if you want results. And I've been getting results. I haven't come outside the first two in a hundred metres breaststroke race for more than three years.

The club coach is Jane Bretell. Dad says she gets right on his nerves. But she's a good coach. She got a bronze in a European final and might have made it to the Sydney Olympics if she hadn't had a knee injury. She says I can get to the Junior National Championships, maybe even international competition. That could mean the Olympics. Who knows? I'm already used to big meets with official times and crowds watching. But I've never been through anything like the last three races. And I'm not just talking about the swimming.

The first race was back in May. I was up against seven lads from different parts of the country, including Ahmed Ali, from Hull, who's beaten me before. It was what's called an "A-grade meet". Sorry. This is boring if you're not into swimming, but it means all of us had already swum the hundred metres breaststroke in one minute 27.2 seconds or better. That's called an "A" time. Anyone who managed to swim faster than one minute 21.8 would go up to a "Double A" time. That's tough. But it was what I was aiming for. If you've got a "Double A" it means you're in the trials for the Junior National Championships.

I was feeling good before the race. I'd stuck to my pre-race routine: pasta four hours before, plenty of water, warm-ups, then getting into the right frame of mind by thinking about what I do best. I got off well too. Right on the B of BANG! It's great when you hit the water with a good start. You're away. All the energy you've been storing up floods out into the pool. Each time you breathe you see the lights and hear the crowd.

Because of her work, Mum hardly ever makes it

to my races. It's Dad who has always come. And usually, after a race, I'll go back and stay with him. Seeing that Dad thinks swimming is boring and the other mums and dads are all stuck-up, he's been a big support. He's come right the way up to Manchester and Loughborough and places and, when I'm in the pool, he really gets behind me.

I could hear him shouting right from the start that night.

"COME ON MART! MOVE IT!"

I didn't rush though. Jane gets me to follow a race-plan, and that means a slowish start. There are four lengths in a hundred metres race. For the first two, I just stay with the others. I find my rhythm but keep something in the bank. It's only down the third length that I go for it.

I got a pretty good turn into the third length.

"THAT'S IT MART!" I heard Dad shout. "SHOW THEM WHAT YOU'RE MADE OF!"

My legs and shoulders were starting to hurt, and there was still half the race to swim, but something happens to me down the third length. Jane calls it "going up a gear" but that's not what it feels like. It's more like losing your head. Something wild takes over. I'm in this world of water, air and sound. Dad's shouting. The others are kicking and reaching around me. And I get this animal feeling. My eyes narrow, my teeth grit and I just claw through the water.

I tore right down the middle of that length and I knew I was closing down on the lads at the front. If I was first to turn into the last length I was sure I'd win it. But at least one of the others turned with me. So the last length had to be a big one.

From the corner of my eye I could see it was Ahmed Ali who was up with me. And he'd got a good turn.

"COME ON MART!" yelled Dad. "**KICK! KICK!**"

And I did. I kicked and reached and kicked and reached. I wasn't going to let Ahmed Ali get away. Halfway down the length, I edged up to him. Then I was past. He came back at me, but I could see the wall. Four more strokes. My hands were on it. I'd won.

I dropped back into the water looking up at the clock. MARTYN SPILLER. First. One minute 21.4. I'd taken almost two seconds off my personal best. It was a "Double-A" time. I was in the trials for the National Championships. I put my hands in the air to salute the crowd. But that was when I realized nobody was even looking at me. They were looking at Dad. Some other spectator had told him to sit down and it had turned into a slanging match. One of the race officials was keeping them apart, but Dad was shouting at the other man and trying to push his way past.

Some of the lads with me in the pool were grinning, and Jane was rushing over. I got out of the water and went across too. I remember hearing Jane say, "Mr Spiller! This is embarrassing for the club!"

Then Dad turned on her.

"I don't give a tinker's toot about the club!" he said.

"Well you're absolutely no help to Martyn if you can't even behave like an adult!" she snapped.

"Who said I'm here to help?" Dad asked her.

Jane gave a tut.

"I think your attitude is quite *inappropriate*!" she said.

"And I think your face is quite like a *dead fish*!" Dad told her.

You always know where you are with Dad. Sometimes he says things you can't help laughing at. Sometimes he loses his head. I tried to step in that night, but it didn't help. Next thing he was pushing past the race official and striding towards the exit, pointing and mouthing off at the man who'd told him to sit down.

Jane walked me back to the changing rooms. She told me twice she'd never seen me swim as well. She said she wanted me to start getting in the right frame of mind for the trials for the Nationals straight away. She told me to forget all about the scene with Dad. I tried. But, in the changing rooms, the other lads wanted to know who the punk bloke was. I said he was my dad. Some of them looked as though they thought I was winding them up. Some of them said they wished their dads were like that. I told them I'd be happy to swap.

I found Dad outside the changing rooms leaning on the wall. I know that frustrated look of his. It's as though he's trying to yawn but can't. I've seen a lot of it recently. First things hadn't worked out with my mum. Then he'd tried to set up a business laying crazy paving and that hadn't been much success. He'd bought an old ice-cream van to drive his tools about in. But he'd hardly got any work.

Dad nodded and ran his tongue around his mouth.

"You coming back with me to Biscuit's?" he asked.

"Suppose so," I said.

"Thought you might want to have tea and a sticky bun with that snooty coach of yours."

"She's all right," I tutted.

"She wouldn't smile if her life depended on it," Dad sniffed.

We walked down the steps and out into the street.

"And as for that prat who told me to sit down," he went on, "he can go and stick his head down the bog!"

Dad led me round to the old ice-cream van in the car-park. "*JIMMY SPILLER CRAZY PAVING*" it said down the side. He unlocked the door.

"Anyway, you won…" he said, getting in.

"I've got a Double A time," I told him. "It means I'm going to be invited to the trials for the Nationals in a few weeks."

Dad started up the engine.

"Well, with all the bloody training you put in, you should be winning everything in sight, Mart," he told me. Then he pushed a tape into the player. There weren't any speakers inside the van. The music came out of the megaphone thing up on the top. And it was turned up really loud. The Pogues came booming out across the car park.

"Turn it down, Dad!" I said.

"No."

"It's too loud."

"It's to celebrate," he said, driving off with a little smile.

The van rolled slowly up the road. It's got a top speed of about twelve miles an hour. Loads of people were coming out of the Sports Hall, and all their heads turned.

"Do you *always* have to act the fool?" I asked, turning the tape player off.

"I'm enjoying that," said Dad. And he switched it back on. "Best live band ever. Me and Biscuit used to go ballistic at their gigs!"

"Will you shut up?" I said. "I just swam the best time

of my life and all you do is make a prat of yourself."

Dad peered through the windscreen.

"I just got into a scrap," he said.

"Well why did you get into a scrap?" I asked. "I've never seen anyone else get into a scrap at a swimming race."

"Perhaps they should do. It would do that coach of yours a power of good. She looks as though she just sat on a garden rake."

"So do you," I muttered.

"I turn up, don't I?" Dad shrugged. "Do I have to be one of those pointy-headed fathers sitting there going on about whether the lane-ropes are tight enough? I don't know about that stuff."

I looked at him.

"You don't have to be like them but…"

"Look, just take it easy can't you?" interrupted Dad. "You're a great swimmer."

"Yeah, and no thanks to you," I told him.

This time it was Dad who turned the music off.

"You know it's about time you stopped taking yourself so seriously," he said. "All you've got to talk about is how good you are at swimming. The only time I spend more than ten minutes with you is when I come to see you in a race. What about lightening up a bit? What about us having a weekend without spending half of it at the Sports

Hall? Couldn't we talk about something except for bloody swimming? You can't spend the rest of your life underwater. You're not a fish."

We turned off the main road. I shrugged.

"Jane says if I believe in myself I can go all the way to the top."

"Well Jane's your coach," said Dad. "She's going to tell you that stuff. But it doesn't work like that!"

"How would you know?" I asked. "You've never won anything. You've never even tried."

We pulled up outside Biscuit's place. Dad turned off the engine but he didn't get out. He looked at me.

"I've never tried?"

"When have you tried?" I asked. "What do you do in this van? You don't get any work! You just drive about with a load of tools in the back."

"Well what do you expect me to have in the back?" asked Dad. "A load of bananas?"

He bit his teeth together like he does sometimes when he's listening to music. I could feel myself doing it too.

"And before you tell me I don't try," he went on, "don't forget I've been in a band for twenty years. I've tried at that. And I had plenty of self-belief when we started. But I found out self-belief doesn't just *make* you a success, whatever your coach tells you!"

I shook my head.

"Your band's never been a success because it's a bunch of old men playing old music no one's interested in any more. It's a losers' band."

"And you're a winner are you?" asked Dad.

"I was tonight!" I told him.

Dad got out of the van and pulled on his jacket. I got my bag and followed him up the steps. He pushed the key in the door of the flat and gave it a shove. Then he turned round.

"Why don't you just go home?" he said. "You don't even like it here."

I tried to ignore him and go in. But there was a really poisonous look in Dad's eyes.

"You don't like it here do you?" he repeated.

"No!" I told him.

"Then don't stay here!" he shouted.

He stood there.

"Don't stay here!" he shouted, right in my face.

It frightened me. But I didn't show it.

"Jane's right," I told him. "You need to grow up."

"Yeah," said Dad. "You and her know it all!"

I started to walk away.

"Biscuit and I have a good time here!" Dad shouted after me. "We write songs! We have a laugh! And those are things your coach and you don't know anything about!"

I didn't say anything, but Dad's voice kept

booming after me.

"And I tell you, that's the last time I see you swim! I've had enough of it!"

I walked off down the pavement waiting to hear the door slam. But it didn't. It just clicked shut.

So that was what happened the night I swam the best race I'd ever swum. I got home, wrote a note for Mum so she would know what was happening. Then I made myself something to eat and got some sleep.

Usually I have a lie-in on Sundays. But I woke up first thing the next morning and I knew I couldn't sleep any more. There was this sharp feeling inside me. It felt as though everything Dad had shouted was in my stomach. I couldn't remember him ever getting that angry with me. I stared at the curtains. Bits of the race and what we'd said went round in my head.

When Mum got up she told me how sick of Dad she was. And both of us sat there complaining about him. Then she asked about the race. It was good to change the subject.

I was tired, but I made it to the pool for training at the end of the day. I always do. Jane brushed aside the whole thing with Dad. You could tell she wanted to concentrate on the swimming.

"Your father just got carried away," she told me.

"Well I wish he'd got carried further away," I

joked, getting into the pool.

It was a regular training session: starts and turns, fast lengths with breaks, then half an hour in the gym. The sun was out as I walked back. I was feeling a lot better than I had in the morning. I felt like swimming so well that Dad would have to shut up. Then a voice called out,

"MART! ALL RIGHT?"

It was Biscuit. He was standing at the bus-stop in a blue T-shirt. It said "JESUS IS COMING – LOOK BUSY".

Biscuit is the drummer in "Bucket of Snot". The rest of the time he works on the checkout at Sainsbury's. His real name is Garry but he's hardly got any hair so Dad started calling him Garry-baldy. That became Biscuit. Don't worry if you don't get it. It's just Dad's sense of humour.

"Been swimming?" Biscuit grinned.

"Yeah," I nodded. "How are you?"

"All right," said Biscuit.

"What about Dad?" I asked. "Is he okay?"

Biscuit gave a funny shrug.

"Not really," he said. "We had a bust up, me, Trevor and him. We were rehearsing this afternoon and he got all serious about this new song. He wanted to play a solo, but so did Trevor. Then your dad just lost his rag. You should see his guitar. It's all smashed."

"Who smashed it?" I asked.

"He did," said Biscuit. "He tried to hit me with it. But I dodged and he hit the wall. Then he smashed it up. He kept on hitting it against the fridge. You should see my fridge door. It's all dented up."

I could feel my heart sinking.

"Is he okay now?" I asked.

"He went out," shrugged Biscuit, holding out his arm for a bus. "He said, 'That's the end of Bucket of Snot. We've played our last song.' Then he drove off in the van."

The bus pulled in and Biscuit got on.

"That's rock'n'roll," he smiled. "Happens all the time."

Mum had left some food out and already gone off to work. After training there's this warm glow in your legs and your arms. It's good just to crash out in front of the telly. And that's what I did. I tried to put all the stuff with Dad out of my mind. But it was no good. I couldn't help wondering how he was. Dad loved that guitar of his. Even if everything around him was in a mess he'd always be tuning it, wiping it clean or putting it carefully into in its case.

The next evening the phone rang. I was up in my room. Mum answered it. From the way her voice went dry, I could tell it was Dad.

"I'm fine," Mum said.

There was a long silence. Then she said, "No, it wouldn't be all right. Now you've moved out it's got to stay like that and you've got to start looking after yourself."

So Dad was asking her if he could come back home.

"I don't care how long it's for," I heard Mum snap.

Then there was another long silence and her voice changed.

"Well I'm glad about that," she told him.

Dad started saying something else. Mum walked through to the living room and shut the door. But I could still just about hear.

"He doesn't," she told him. "If you want to know he's sick to the back teeth of you… and the way you embarrass him."

She listened to Dad for a while longer. Then she said, "No, Jimmy. What he needs is you to get your act together. That's what we all need."

They went on for a bit longer and I could hear Mum's voice getting angry. Then she was clunking the phone back in the hall and filling the kettle in the kitchen.

When I came down she told me Dad had called.

"How is he?" I asked.

"He says he's getting a job," said Mum with a nod. "Let's hope it works out."

I trained really hard over the next couple of weeks. The trials for the Nationals were going to be on the first Saturday in June at the International Swimming Centre across town. Jane wanted me to swim in one more race before then. So she put me down for an Open Meet up in Luton, the Sunday before.

I didn't hear anything from Dad. I thought about going round to see him a couple of times. But I didn't. I told myself it was up to him. Sooner or later he'd have to make touch and then we'd sort things out.

A few of us from Vale Road went to the meet in Luton. Jane organized a minibus. The radio was on and everyone was joking about, even Jane. But I stayed quiet most of the time. I wanted to run through the race-plan in my head.

Luton's a huge place and there was quite a crowd in. I didn't recognize any of the lads I was up against, but Jane had told me none of them had personal bests as good as mine. As we stood by our blocks I glanced at the spectators. I missed seeing Dad there.

The starter signal went. The others went off quicker than I expected. I wanted to keep up, but I didn't want to mess up my race plan. At the first turn, I must have been down in seventh place. Then, as soon as I set off down the second length, something felt wrong. My legs were hurting, and it was early for that. I pushed myself but I was still at the back of the race. There were a lot of voices and cheering. But they weren't for me. Jane watches but she doesn't shout anything. I might have made it up to fifth by the second turn. But I'd say I was four metres behind the lads in front, maybe four and a half.

I threw myself at the turn. Then I bit my teeth and got ready to really give it something down the third length. I needed to up the pace. I did two strokes, three, really big ones and I could feel myself starting to close the gap. But it wasn't right. I didn't have that animal feeling. Dad wasn't shouting. I reached and kicked. My rhythm was good. My shape was good. But I couldn't get myself into that wild mood.

The third length usually flashes past and I find myself at the front of the race. But that night it went on and on. Perhaps I made it up into fourth at one point but I was slipping back again by the turn. And that last length hurt. I kept pushing. But I was way off the front. I didn't have anything left in the tank. I pushed for the end wall with my eyes narrowed, and I slammed my hands down. There was pain right the way through me. I breathed and bobbed in the water and looked up at the board. MARTYN SPILLER. Fifth. One minute 23.6.

On the way home I felt pretty bad. Everyone else had swum well. Jane tried to talk me out of it.

But she was too soothing and nice. I hadn't come in fifth in a race for years and years.

The weather got hot. The days seemed long. The trials were the following Saturday night. Dad never called. And I wanted him to. That argument was still in my stomach. It was like a bruise that you keep squeezing to see if it's still there. Mum never said much about it. But Jane could tell. She asked a few times how things were with Dad. I said I didn't really know. She told me to go round and see him. She said Dad thought the world of me and we'd sort things out. She said if you've got something on your mind it affects your concentration and you won't swim your best. She was right. I knew it. But I didn't go round and see him.

As the week went on I started to get nervous about the trials. It was going to be such a big occasion and it was all going to come down to one race. Whoever came in first, second and third was going to make it through to the Junior National Championships. And it was going to be a really fast race.

After training on the Friday, Jane told me I should get a local paper. She wouldn't tell me why. She just smiled. I bought one at the corner shop and stood in the sunshine, turning the pages. There was football on the back. Then I saw my name.

## LOCAL TEEN SWIM HOPE

*Martyn Spiller, who swims for the Vale Road Swimming Club, will be competing in trials for the Junior National Championships. The International Swimming Centre will host the trials on Saturday 6th June. Thirteen-year-old Spiller achieved a personal-best time to qualify for the trials. His coach Jane Bretell said, "Martyn can go all the way to the top. He is a natural swimmer and he has the attitude that goes with winning."*

I knew everyone was going to love seeing me in the paper. It gave me a lift. But it made me feel even more nervous. I lay in bed that night, determined to get some rest with the trials the next day. But I wasn't sleepy. I was thinking about what it would be like if I won the race. Then I imagined what it would be like if I swam like I had at Luton. Then I started wondering about how Dad was. And what Jane had said was churning round in me. I knew she was right. If I was going to swim my best I needed to sort things out with him.

I did get some sleep, but as soon as I woke up all those feelings came rushing back into me. And I felt really clear. I wanted to swim my best. I really wanted to swim my best. So I was going round to sort things out with Dad. Once I'd decided that I felt a lot better. I got up, had breakfast and thought about what I had to say to him. I even started imagining him coming along to the race that night and cheering me on.

Mum made me my pre-race pasta. Then, when she went off to work, she left me a good-luck card. Jane was going to pick me up at six. So I had time. I opened the front door. It was warm outside. As I headed up the street I knew I was doing the right thing. I found myself walking quickly and I only slowed down when I turned the corner near the flats.

As I went up the steps my head was full of what I was going to say to Dad. I pushed the bell. There were footsteps. The door swung open. It was Biscuit.

"Hello Mart," he nodded.

"Is Dad in?" I asked.

Biscuit shook his head.

"Your dad's gone," he said. "He moved out."

"He moved out?" I said.

"He's renting a place of his own."

"When did he move?" I asked.

"The week before last," said Biscuit. "He got a job delivering vegetables and he's renting his own place."

"I wanted to see him," I said.

Biscuit shrugged.

"Well I don't have the address or anything. But I'll be seeing him. We're going to see The Pogues tonight. They're doing a comeback show. I can pass on a message."

I thought a bit.

"I've got a race tonight," I told him. "I was going to invite Dad if he wants to come."

"It's The Pogues gig tonight, Mart!" grinned Biscuit. "You'll get him along to the swimming another time!"

I nodded.

"Well just tell him that I'd like to see him," I said.

"I'll tell him," Biscuit nodded. "And go easy on that swimming. I hear it's bad for your knees!"

I nodded. Then we said goodbye. And I headed back. I was going to have to do it on my own and every step of the way home I told myself I would.

I didn't mention Dad to Jane when she picked me up. And she didn't ask. She just took me through the things we'd been working on – stroke-length, breath-control, mental attitude. Then we were at the Swimming Centre and everything went in a whirl. I was changing. I was warming-up and I was being called through to the race.

I recognized some of the lads I was up against. Ahmed Ali had made it. We nodded at each other. Then I looked round the gallery. And Dad was sitting there. You couldn't miss him with his red hair. He was sitting at the front with his elbows on his knees. I couldn't believe it.

Our eyes met and he gave me a funny little shrug.

Then he clenched his fist. I grinned and I was so amazed I almost forgot to put my goggles on. I was still adjusting them when they called us to our blocks. Dad had given up going to the gig to come and see me swim. I glanced across at the other lads. Ahmed Ali was standing next to me staring into the water. I could hardly believe what was happening. All I could do was take some deep breaths and wait for the starter signal.

When it came I got off quickly. I felt good. And the pace down the first length was fine. I was right up there at the first turn, ahead of Ahmed Ali. I got a good turn too. But down the second length I felt my energy level just dropping a bit. And the others really upped the pace. I didn't want to go too fast too soon, but I didn't want to get left behind. I could feel them coming past me. And I couldn't hear my dad. He seemed to be just sitting there quietly. There were shouts ringing all around. But I couldn't hear my dad.

I pushed myself to keep up. I gritted my teeth, kicked and reached, I gave it all I could. But I was breathing too fast and I was slipping right to the back of the race. I just hoped I had enough left for a good third length. I did a huge turn and came flying off the end wall. But the others seemed to have got good turns too. I was still at the back of the race and the water felt heavy.

"COME ON MART!" It was Dad. "COME ON SON!"

And something shifted. I breathed and narrowed my eyes and breathed again. Yes. There was still power in me.

**"COME ON SON!"** Dad called again. **"YOU CAN DO IT MART!"**

One stroke, two, three. I was making up ground. I could feel some flow.

**"COME ON MART!"**

It was Jane. I'd never heard her shout before.

**"COME ON MART!"**

They were shouting together. The wild feeling came over me. I clawed at the water. By the end of the length, I'd made it up to fifth place, only inches behind Ahmed Ali. I got a big last turn and Ahmed Ali didn't. I got half a metre on him. I was up into fourth. The leaders were close, but the lads behind me were pretty close too. It was the first three going through to the Nationals. I lashed my arms at the lane. It was as though the weight of the water was helping me now. Dad was shouting. Jane was shouting. I kicked hard, reached, kicked again. I was closing in on third place and the guy in third was fading.

**"COME ON MART!"**

I saw the wall. There was enough water left to get past into third place. But then Ahmed Ali came tearing up on the other side. There was nothing I could do. I went past the lad into third, but Ahmed Ali went past me. His hands were on the wall. And then mine were. I looked up at the board to check. MARTYN SPILLER. Fourth. One minute 21.8.

The crowd were clapping. I caught my breath and Ahmed Ali put an arm round my neck.

"Tough luck, mate," he said, panting.

I felt really disappointed. I'd missed out by a whisker. But I knew I couldn't have swum much better than that. I sank into the water. Ahmed saluted the crowd.

"Hope your dad isn't going to beat me up outside," he grinned.

I shook my head.

"You'll be all right, as long as you go out the back way," I told him. Then I looked across at Dad. He was standing up, clapping with the others.

I congratulated the rest of the lads and clambered out. Dad was coming towards me. He reached out an arm and gave me a hug.

"What are you doing here?" I asked.

"I wanted to cheer you on, didn't I?" said Dad.

"How did you know about it?"

"You were in the paper, Mart," Dad said.

"Did you see that?" I asked.

He nodded.

"I needed to be in the top three to qualify," I told him.

"I know," Dad shrugged. "But that's how it goes."

"Just a couple of tenths of a second faster and I'd have made it."

"Well if you ask me these lane ropes are a shade too tight," Dad said, "I wouldn't be surprised if that slowed you down, Mart."

I looked at him for a moment before I realized he was joking. Then they started announcing the next race and everyone had to clear away from the pool-side.

"I'll drop you home if you want," Dad called.

I nodded back and went off to get changed.

Jane was waiting as I came out.

"I'm sorry Martyn," she said. "But you swam well. You swam your best."

"I put in a pretty good time," I told her.

"You were up against some of the best swimmers in the country."

I nodded.

"There's always next year," I said.

She smiled.

"So things are all right now… with your Dad?"

"Hope so," I told her.

"That's good," she said. "You've done really well considering all you've been through."

"Thanks Jane," I told her. "Thanks for everything."

Dad's van was parked over the road. It looked different inside. He'd tidied it up. And there was a new little stereo. I looked over my shoulder as he started up the engine.

"There's a load of bananas in the back," I said.

Dad nodded and drove off.

"I've got work delivering boxes of organic fruit and veg. I have to put in a lot of hours but I'm doing all right."

I looked at him.

"I haven't even spoken to you for weeks," I said.

"I know," Dad replied. "I had a row with your Mum on the phone the other week. I didn't want to make touch until I'd sorted myself out a bit."

"Biscuit said you'd rented a flat."

Dad nodded.

"What's that like?" I asked.

"Two bedrooms Mart." He nodded. "One for you if you want to come and stay."

He clicked on the stereo. It was Bucket of Snot:

*Playing punk rock is a terrible 'abit!*

*But it beats being hit on the head with a rabbit!*

"Speakers inside," Dad said.

"So has the band split?" I asked.

"Yeah. But I've had a chat with them. We reckon it's a good thing we split because now we can do a comeback gig."

He turned left, away from the Swimming Centre.

"Great song," he nodded.

"You missed going to the Pogues tonight," I said.

"They were probably better the first time round," Dad told me. Then he added, "Listen. I'm sorry about laying into you that night. It's just I was missing seeing you properly. And nothing felt right about us staying at Biscuit's together."

I nodded. Then I said, "I'm sorry about some things I said too. I didn't mean you don't help me with my swimming. You're the one who's always supported me. It's great having you there when I'm racing. I only really got moving tonight when you started shouting."

"You did great," Dad said. "You came right back at them."

I nodded.

"Jane says you keep at it through the hard times and the good times will come."

"Or maybe they won't," shrugged Dad. "And who cares?"

And we drove off at 12 miles an hour, listening to the song.

# Twenty Crows

## RON KOERTGE

I walked my dad to the Subaru, which he patted like it was a pony. "Six thousand miles a month on this baby." Then he slid in and reached for the frayed seat belt. "Why," he asked, "do you dress like that?"

I looked down at myself: grubby sneaks, pants cut off just below the knee and my favourite T-shirt with NOBODY'S PERFECT on it. Fat red braces hid a couple of the letters. "Like what?" I asked innocently.

His index finger came out and tapped my chest. "What's that supposed to mean?"

"It's a band."

"You're kidding."

"Like you've got a sense of humour."

"Don't give me attitude, Peter. If you're mad about last night, say so."

"Okay, I'm mad about last night."

"I told you, I got held up. I said I was sorry."

"You always get held up, and you're always sorry."

"I've got responsibilities. You don't have any idea what it's like to—" Just then his phone played its stupid tune. I turned and started for the house. My father leaned out the car window.

"We'll talk," he bellowed. "Just. . . not now. I'll call you. I mean I'll see you tonight. No, wait. Not tonight."

I kept walking. But I could hear my dad making promises to whoever was on the phone. "For sure," he said. "Not a problem. I'll be there. You can depend on me."

Yeah, right.

Inside my mother tried to cover for him, "He's sorry about the game. Really he is."

"How do you know that? Did he call or leave a note?"

"Peter, your father works hard so we can have nice things."

"I didn't ask for nice things, did you?"

My mom held one arm out, but if I gave in and let her pat me it'd mean everything was all right. And everything wasn't all right.

👫 👫 👫

Five minutes later, I glided up Chicago Street on my bike. Bruno, Kevin's father's partner, stood beside his new SUV. He wore blue rubber gloves and held a bucket of soapy water.

Two fathers. How weird was that? And, according to my mom, one very confused mother in Miami.

"He's around back," Bruno said without looking

up from the fender he was all but fondling. Bruno always wore jeans and boots. He was a landscape architect, but he dressed like a lumberjack.

Sure enough, Kevin was sweeping the patio that not only looked like something out of a magazine, it **was** something out of a magazine. One called *Leisure Living*. Everybody in the neighbourhood had passed around that big picture of Bruno smiling and Kevin's dad pretending to rake the Zen garden.

"I wish," Kevin said poking at the smooth sand, "about a thousand cats would sneak in here and poo."

"That's what I like to hear: the true spirit of Zen."

"A guy could lose his mind in this place. Last night they had dinner then brandy by the koi pond, tonight they'll have dinner then brandy by the koi pond. Why do I have to be there?"

I growled, "Don't you have homework?"

Kevin laughed, because that's what one of his fathers always said. "Well, yeah, if you call homework trying to log onto Naked Girls in Cowboy Hats dot com."

I tugged at the handlebars of my red Huffy. "Let's go get XJ."

Kevin shook his head. "He has to wash the car, do the dishes, clean his room, paint the house and stop racial discrimination in the workplace. And now he's grounded because somebody stole his bike."

"Well, that blows."

"His dad just went ballistic. You know how he is."

Actually everybody knows how XJ's dad is – way over the top. For his last birthday XJ wanted a bicycle, okay? What he got was all the parts of a bicycle. And no how-to sheet either. If he wanted a bike, his father said, he would have to put it together. That way he would learn something too.

"What's XJ going to do?" I asked.

"Probably grow a beard. He's not getting out of the house until he's forty-two."

When Kevin's mobile rang, he dug it out of his cargo pants pocket and read the message. "Theo says to meet at Norman's. Let's go."

*♀*♂*♀*♂*♀

Twenty minutes later we were all (except XJ) on Norman's porch waiting for Mark. We watched him slow down as he got closer, make lazy figure eights in front of the house, then stop.

"Oh, my god," said Theo. "If it isn't the mascot for the Miami Citrus All Stars."

Mark yelled from the curb, "Don't even start."

He was in orange from head to toe. Well, from neck to toe actually because he had this green hat that looked like a stem.

"It was either put this on," Mark explained, "or stay in the house."

"Tough call," Theo observed, finally cracking

everybody up.

Mark stalked towards us. "I tell my dad, 'I'm not a jock, I'll never be a jock, I don't want to be a jock.' He says, 'You've got the genes. Dress like one and you will be.' How retarded is that? I was a pirate for Halloween. Did I say, 'Yo ho ho'? Did I make people walk the plank? I'm no athlete. All I do is get hit in the wotsits by grounders and get my nose broken by footballs."

"And," said Kevin, "pee your pants at the free-throw line."

"Exactly. I could dress in these stupid warm-up/cool-down/glow-in-the-dark outfits until I was ninety and I'd never be co-ordinated. I think there was a mix-up at the hospital and somewhere there's a kid with 'Super Jock' on his T-shirt and a dad with a library card. Damn it!" Mark wadded up the green hat and stuffed it in a zippered pocket.

Norman got to his feet. "C'mon. Maybe my dad can help."

"Hold it a second, Mark." Theodore took a picture with his new camera, the one his dad bought him, the one Theo nicknamed the Guiltflix Special. Theo took pictures of almost everything. Mark – who liked words a lot more than sports – called him our documentarian.

All of us had been friends forever, and we planned to be friends forever. Thanks to Theo, we could get together at thirty and see what we'd been like at twelve. When we planned the reunion it was just going to be the six of us. We would sit down in our grown-up bodies and look at the photographs Theo brought along.

Norman held the screen door. "It's okay," he said. "Nobody's home."

Norman's mom, Mrs Pavlic, didn't have to work because she got a lot of money after her husband died. But she volunteered at the North Point Hospital or Main Street Mission, so the bungalow on Chicago Street where Norman lived was pretty much ours. He had a sister who was supposed to keep an eye on him, but she was spacey and had a lot of boyfriends, so she didn't. Not that it mattered, because the six of us were almost always together. And we looked out for each other.

We filed down to the rec room with its Elton John pinball machine, regulation pool table and old-fashioned juke box. Mr Pavlic, Norman's father, had been a good dancer, a killer pool player and trick shot artist and a mad collector of snow domes. He had two hundred and twenty-nine of those things. They all had something inside, like an Eiffel tower or a palm tree or a mountain. There were usually little people standing around in a blizzard.

We knew we could touch any of the snow

domes, but we didn't. They belonged to Mr Pavlic.
The whole place did actually. Norman's mother
never wanted her son to forget his father, so she had
about a million pictures of him: standing by one of
the Cadillacs he sold for a living, hugging her and a
jitterbug trophy or lying on a striped towel by a blue
pool. He was, Mark said, ubiquitous. I looked it up,
and he was right. Mr Pavlic was everywhere – every
wall and mantle, bookcase and end table. Even in the
kitchen. Even in the bathroom.

We were used to all that, though, so we just sat
around the card table with the felt surface that was fun
to pet and waited for Norman to talk to his dad's ghost.

We were just about to get started when Theo's
mobile went off. He put his camera down, flipped
the phone open, glanced at the message and showed
it to us.

It said: I Love You, son.

"Doesn't it," Theo asked, "just make you all
warm inside?"

"At least," I reminded him, "he talks."

"But he doesn't, not really. He types. He divorces
my mom, has a whole other family, but text-messages
me some Valentine's Day rubbish."

Norman held out his hands to the guys on either
side of him. "We'll ask my dad about that too."

Mark couldn't wait. "I'm first. I'm the one dressed

like a tropical fruit."

Kevin frowned. "Strictly speaking neither Florida nor California is in the tropics."

Mark's eyes narrowed. "'The tropics.' Well, aren't you Mr Geography."

Norman gave him a look. "Cut it out, you guys. You go first Mark, then Theo. And don't worry. My father's got all the time in the world."

He took two or three deep breaths, closed his beady eyes. All of us were at that in-between stage which my mother calls "all feet and ears". Norman was that and kind of ratty-looking too. And he wasn't very good at much. Not school, not sports, not anything, really. Talking to his dead father, that's what he was good at.

"Dad?" he said. "How are you? What's the news from heaven today?" Norman always talked about heaven first, just to get warmed up. Last time we learned that the snakes up there didn't slither. They rode scooters.

So Norman listened, then grinned. He looked at us and announced, "There are new lambs to tend, but the kangaroos are a big help."

Mark squirmed. "C'mon, get to the point."

"Dad," Norman said, "Mark's got a problem he'd like to run by you."

Mark didn't wait for an okay. He blurted, "Can

you see me from heaven, Mr Pavlic? Can you see how I'm dressed?"

Norman nodded, "Yes. I can see everything from up here."

"Well, what's my dad thinking? I'm no jock. Why does he do this stuff to me?"

Norman's voice changed. It got deeper, more raspy, more like Mr Pavlic's when he was alive. "Do you realize how strong you are, Mark?"

Mark scowled. "Get serious. I'm the one who can't do a chin-up."

"Every day your dad wants you to be something you're not, and every day you resist. He pushes you, you push back."

Mark snorted. "He pushes. You've got that right."

Norman smiled as he said, "And you resist. It's like isometrics for your soul. That's why every day you get stronger."

Mark squirmed, then frowned. He let go of Kevin's hand long enough to pull at the sleeve of his warm-up jacket. He inspected his thin, pale forearm. "Does this look strong to you?"

"Just remember," said Norman, "your dad thinks he's a failure."

"Are you kidding? He was Mr Everything in college."

"And," Norman rasped, "he got cut every time

he tried out for the pros. You have ten times more inner strength than your father. Theo does too. It's not easy living with just your mom, Theo, but look how well you're doing."

Theo looked surprised. Apparently it was his turn. He leaned toward Norman. "I am?"

"Everybody knows you are. When your dad left, you really stepped up. Your mother couldn't get along without you."

"I don't know about that. She's got a lot of friends now."

"But they're just friends, Theodore. You're the one she depends on."

Theo frowned. "So I've got inner strength too."

"Absolutely."

Norman blinked and asked in his usual voice, "Who's next?"

We all looked at each other. "Well, this is no biggie," said Kevin, "but what should a guy do if he doesn't have his homework and somebody smart offers to let me copy his. Him, I mean. Offers to let him copy his."

Norman repeated the question solemnly, then replied, "Dad says he should be honest. That he should tell his teacher he forgot and ask if he can make the assignment up. If not, learn from that mistake and do better next time."

"How about when I have weird thoughts?" asked Mark.

Norman asked, waited, then announced. "Not weird. Unique. Life wouldn't be very interesting if everybody had the same thoughts."

Who wouldn't like Norman's dad? We could talk to him about stuff that would've made our real fathers mad. Or totally suspicious.

Norman was getting back into the heavenly kangaroo thing again when Theo said, "Tell your dad thanks, and then let's do something. Get a Coke. Go somewhere."

I could tell Norman didn't like that. "Sit tight, you guys," he said. And he held up one wait-a-minute finger.

Kevin looked at me and rolled his eyes but that stopped when Norman announced, "You won't believe this! Dad says XJ's bike is down by the arroyo. Behind some bushes just past the glass house."

That was great news! If XJ got his bike back, maybe he wouldn't be grounded any more.

Mark was already on his feet. "I get to tell him!"

"No way," said Norman. "My father found it." And he shot up the stairs.

We rocketed down the street towards XJ's big brown house with the shake roof.

He was sweeping the driveway when we powered

up. Mark and Norman fell all over themselves with the news.

"Are you serious?" he said.

Norman assured him, "I'm totally serious. My dad said so."

"Who stole it in the first place?"

"Dad didn't say. It doesn't matter. What matters is that it's there."

Already XJ was looking to see how much work was left. "Well, if it's not and my dad comes home for lunch and I'm gone, I'm toast. Or since I'm already toast, I'll be croutons."

"It'll only take twenty minutes," said Kevin. "Put that stupid broom down."

Everybody scrambled for their bikes. XJ rode double with me. We went straight to the arroyo, past the glass house and right to the bushes just beyond. Norman knew exactly where to go.

And there was the bike, lying on its side with its handle bars twisted around and sticking up so it kind of looked a dead deer. Right where Norman's father said it would be.

👫👫👫

Sure, we talked about it. Who wouldn't? I even told my dad while I walked him to the car in the morning, a one-minute ritual that Kevin called "an orgy of intimacy".

Dad just stared at me. "You don't actually believe that, do you, Peter?"

My father wore a blue short-sleeved shirt and a clip-on tie. He looked tired and harassed and it wasn't even eight o'clock in the morning. Who would want to do what he did – grow up, have a wife and kid you almost never saw and then sell stuff? I finally answered his question, "Kind of. How did Norman know where it was if his dad didn't tell him?"

"Oh, for crying out loud, Pete. The kid's a thief." He glanced at his watch. "We'll talk about this tonight, okay?"

*Yes, sir. Whatever you say, sir. You can depend on me, sir. I'll wait by the door with my leash in my mouth.*

I rode over to Mark's and walked right into the kitchen because almost nobody on Chicago Street locked their doors. Mark was somewhere inside a set of Green Bay Packers sweats. Kevin was already telling the bike story. Megan – Mark's oldest sister and if you ask me the one who could have been in the *Guiness Book of Records* as Most Exasperated Girl in the World – stood at the stove flipping pancakes. When Kevin was finished, she waved the spatula at us, "Why don't you pathetic nematodes be a little more naïve and gullible. Norman's such a needy little dork that he stole XJ's bike so he could tell everybody where it was and be a hero for fifteen seconds."

We – Kevin and Mark and I – glanced at each other. "You're as nuts as my dad," I said. "Norman wouldn't do something like that."

She tried her glance-of-withering scorn on me as she threatened her brother. "And just wait until I tell Mom. No way is she going to let you hang around a lying little spaz like Norman." She slid the big plate with the last of the pancakes onto the table, tossed the spatula into the sink and headed for her room. "God," she said, "I can't wait to get out of this house!"

Kevin put down his fork, "Speaking of who can't hang with who, my dads said they'd prefer me to see less of Norman. How gay do you have to be to say *prefer*?"

"My one straight dad," I said, "is going to talk to me about Norman later but since later means never, who cares?"

"So," said Kevin. "I prefer to see Norman constantly."

That night all the guys were at my house. Dad wasn't home yet (what a shock!). My mom came out of the kitchen, looped her arms around Norman's neck, looked him right in the eye and said, "You found XJ's bike. Good for you."

Then she kissed him on the forehead and turned away. We were in the living room stretched out like a bunch of lazy cats when Norman said, "Feel how warm it just got in here? It's Rachel."

I hoped my mom hadn't heard that but it was too late. She rushed in, looked around like something was on fire and the next thing I knew she was crying so hard she had to go lie down.

I took hold of Norman's skinny arm. "Now look what you did. I told you not to talk about my sister."

"Dad says Rachel's fine. Just not completely committed to the other world."

"You know my mom's trying not to think about her. Don't be a jerk."

"My father says she has to process her grief. Not thinking about Rachel isn't going to help. He also says to tell your mother to take lots of vitamin C. Her immune system is compromised and she's very vulnerable."

"Oh, shut up, Norman."

The very next day, my mother came down with such a bad flu that I got scared and called my dad who called Bruno who drove us to Urgent Care and I promised to not let her out of my sight; otherwise she would have to check into the hospital.

When Dad finally got home, I told him what Norman's father said about vulnerability and vitamin C, and he said, "That's enough of this rubbish. It's not funny any more. Somebody's got to talk to that kid's mother."

Dad was heating some soup for Mom and I was

trying to study when Norman called. I told him, "I'm not talking to you, man. That thing about Rachel was cold. You got my mother all upset and now she's sick."

The only thing he said was this: "My father wants everybody to know that tonight stones will fall from the sky."

Then he hung up.

Oh, man. Mr Pavlic used to tell us normal stuff like when it was going to rain or the Cubs might win the pennant. Now he's finding stolen bikes and sounding like Chicken Little.

What was I supposed to do – blow Norman off and have half the neighbourhood get a concussion, or tell my father and have him give me one?

I didn't want to, but I trudged downstairs.

Dad started shouting almost before I was finished. "Stones from the sky? Are you nuts?"

"But what if he's right?"

"Look, I'll talk to Theo's dad and XJ's dad and everybody else's dad and we'll get this straightened out. Son of a gun! This kind of aggravation I don't need."

Well, whether he needed it or not, he got it because next morning we were all standing around staring at what was left of the windshield on Bruno's SUV. And at the monster stone lying on the hood.

"See!" said Kevin, "Just like Norman said." But his

father told him to shut up. "This isn't a message from the spirit world. This is harassment. It happens to gay people all the time."

XJ's father took a turn. "Absolutely." He shook his finger at all of us. "I want you kids to stop this mumbo-jumbo."

Theo just took pictures of the smashed window and of the egg-shaped rocks lying all over the place.

My friends and I could hardly wait to get to Norman's. Downstairs the snow domes were all upside down and something far out was playing on the juke box. Some non-song. Something that wasn't music.

"Twenty crows," Norman chanted sitting at the table by himself and not even waiting for us to make a circle. "There will be exactly twenty dead crows on the ground tomorrow morning. And then everybody will know that they should listen to my father."

Now what? Partly I wanted it to be true because it would be kind of cool. But mostly I wanted it not to be true because things were getting very strange. It's fun to believe in ghosts; you just play along. But this thing with Norman wasn't fun any more.

🕴🕴🕴🕴🕴

By seven-thirty the next morning, everyone was out of their houses on Chicago Street staring at the dead crows on XJ's lawn, and at XJ's father who was listening to Mark's father. The sun was barely up but he was dressed like he'd just signed a contract with Nike. Hat on backwards, diamond stud in his left ear and three-hundred-dollar shoes. He was saying that a few dead birds didn't mean anything. Wild animals died all the time; it was just natural.

"You're telling me," said XJ's father, "that all those black birds laid out in a line like that on a black man's lawn don't mean anything? If you believe that, you're as stupid as you look. This is a hate crime, just like the rock through that homo's windshield."

"No, it isn't," said XJ, "it's magic. Norman's dad knew where my bike was. He knew exactly how many crows there'd be."

"Sure he knew," my father said, "because Norman stole the bike and put it down there and last night he killed those poor crows."

XJ's father snarled. "That's right, and I'm not waiting around until he burns somebody's house down and then claims his daddy made him do it." He headed for Norman's. Everybody did.

My friends and I watched our parents fill up the porch of the shingled bungalow. XJ's father was first, the other fathers behind him, the mothers clustered around the porch swing. Theo's mom even sat down in it and lit the first cigarette of the day.

But I edged forwards and leaned in when Norman's mother opened the door.

"We want to see that son of yours," XJ's father demanded. "We want to know what the hell he thinks he's doing with this séance business and we especially want to know where he was last night."

I heard her answer through the screen door. "He was with me," she said. "I've been ill and he sat up in a chair in case I needed anything. He's asleep now and I won't have you disturbing him. I don't know what this is all about, but he's a good boy. He always has been. You're not going to talk to him, and if you want to talk to me you'll have to come back later." Then she doubled over coughing and closed the door.

Everyone just stood there frozen until Theo's mother gave a little snort, flicked her cigarette onto the lawn, went right to her son and led him away. Then everybody's mom did the same thing, and pretty soon the fathers clomped down the steps too.

＊＊＊＊＊

That night Norman called Kevin. Kevin told Mark who called Theo who got a hold of XJ who text-messaged me, so I just gave up and took my life in my hands.

I rang my dad, "Norman says all the lights on Chicago Street will go out at exactly nine o'clock tonight."

First he didn't say anything. Then just three words: "I'll be there." And he hung up.

That's why everybody was outside right after the sun went down. All the husbands and wives, the sisters and daughters, even Bruno's dog which was little and bald and shivered all the time. All of them agreeing that Norman hadn't had adequate role models.

They thought they were so smart, but they didn't know anything. We knew which plants in the arroyo you could eat. When we camped out down there, sometimes all of us had the same dream. There was this one coyote we'd taught to eat out of our hands. *Adequate role models*. That's the kind of rubbish grown-ups got from watching television. And even if it was true, it was as much our fault as anybody's. Norman ran with us. *We* were his role models.

When it was almost time, Norman led his mother onto the porch, kind of gallantly holding the door, then giving her his arm on the warped steps. Everyone watched them negotiate the sidewalk the tree roots had broken, the same roots we used to pretend were boa constrictors.

As they got closer to us, everybody quieted down. Norman walked to the middle of the street by himself. He lifted both arms, and in that yellow shirt made a kind of glowing Y. Both eyes were shut tight. Seconds passed, then a minute. Then more minutes.

Every light on Chicago Street blazed. Norman started to shiver. My mom took a step towards him but Dad stopped her. He walked up to Norman instead, "It's five minutes after nine, son, and just about as bright out here as it can get. Now I want you to tell us why you broke that windshield and slaughtered those birds? You don't have to be afraid. You did a stupid thing, but we're still your friends and neighbours."

Norman's shivers turned to shudders right before he passed out. He didn't fall sideways like a tower. He just kind of folded up. People ran towards him, two or three phones lit up. The mothers fussed over him; the fathers looked at each other.

When Norman finally had a little colour back, his mom helped him to his house. Everybody else just wandered around and looked dazed.

My dad slumped onto the curb then looked up at me. "That kid has got some screwed-up imagination."

"Maybe," I said, "he just likes being with his dad."

"Petey," my father said. "Mr Pavlic is dead. You know that."

"Maybe I do," I blurted, "but he talks to Norman more than you ever talk to me."

My father took a deep breath, then let it out slowly. "I'm not very good at this, am I?"

I wasn't going to let him off that easy. "Not very good at what?"

He looked everywhere but at me. "You know

why I work so hard?"

"So Mom and I can have nice things we don't want?"

He shook his head. "I couldn't sleep last night, so I figured out that I can put money away for your college and buy your mom that dryer she needs and get home earlier too. Would you like that?"

I sat down beside him. "Are you kidding? Sure."

"Then that's how it'll be. Starting tomorrow. Or next week. Definitely next week."

I'm not sure I believed him, but I liked feeling his hand on my shoulder because he almost never did that.

It was only a little miracle, but my friends didn't get to see it. Kevin was busy listening to his fathers. Mark stood beside his sister and his gung-ho dad, XJ by his dad whose big arm hung across his shoulders like a yoke. Theo leaned on his mother, his camera hanging from his wrist.

# The Journey to Ompah

## Tim Wynne-Jones

My Dad is so polite his pants catch on fire. Okay, just the once. And it was the bird's fault, a bird that had no business being in this part of the world. Then again, you have to wonder... If it hadn't been for the bird and the cute reporter and the burning trousers...

But let me start at the beginning. Let me take you there.

* * * * *

The whole weird trip starts on a beautiful mid-summer morning. The blazing pants are still hours away. I'm sitting at the kitchen table checking out the movies in the newspaper. I have a date tonight. I wonder if maybe Dad does, too. He's washing a purple shirt in the sink. Except he isn't really washing it, he's watching it. Just leaning on the counter as if he isn't sure what to do next. I've noticed that a lot lately.

"It won't wash itself, Dad."

He tosses me a smile two sizes too small. He says, "According to the directions, it will." Then he holds up a pink bottle, *Feathery Soft for Delicates*. It makes me think of Mom's stuff hanging in the bathroom. Only not our bathroom any more.

"It's silk," he says. "Doesn't like to get roughed up."

Just then the timer on his wristwatch buzzes and he returns to his delicate task. I observe. Since the break-up, I've been observing him a lot. When I'm at Mom's I observe her. I'm trying to figure out how we got to this trial separation thing. How, six weeks ago, just plain here became here and there.

*"He's too polite, that papa of yours."*

I watch him rinse the shirt out under cold water.

*I open up the dictionary and I say to Mom, "Polite as in having good manners or polite as in refined, cultivated?" She screws up her face. "He has always been the perfect gentleman, of course. But lately, he's... how should I say... intimidé. He's nervous all the time as if he was having an affair."*

*"But he isn't."*

*She shrugs. Pouts. "He's too finicky," she says.*

Gingerly, he wrings out his shirt. Is this what she means?

*I look up Finicky. "So he concentrates too much on small and unimportant details?"*

*"Michel," she says, frowning. "Enough with the dictionary."*

*"I'm trying to understand."*

*She wraps her arms around herself. She looks as if she's trying to understand as well, leaning on her own counter in her own kitchen.*

*"Suddenly it is, 'everything in moderation,' she says. But this… This contrainte. This is not moderation. It is…" But language fails her. Two languages fail her.*

I watch him slowly wrap his fragile shirt in a fluffy yellow towel.

*"'Moderation: the limiting, controlling, or restricting of something so that it becomes or remains moderate.' And that's bad?"*

*Now she glares. "He wasn't always like this, Michel. Just the last year or so." She pours herself a glass of wine. "Everything in moderation is fine. But you have to moderate moderation with a little joie de vivre, non?" She sips the wine. "He used to be a passionate man, your father."*

*I close the dictionary: I don't want any more definitions. But I lie in bed later that night tying to think what happened in the last year or so to change things. I became a teenager. Is it me?*

Dad stands back and regards his handiwork, pleased with himself in a modest kind of way.

The phone rings. He picks it up and his eyes get big. "No!" he says. And I am rigid with fear. Something has happened to Mom. But now I see that his eyes are big with wonder not alarm. "You're kidding!" he says. Wonder transforms his face to a grin the size of July. "Really?" he says. "*Archilocus alexandri?*"

I should have guessed. It's about a bird.

"What now?" I ask. "Someone spot a dodo walking up Yonge Street?"

He shakes his head. "Nothing so large," he says. "But rare. A black-chinned Hummingbird."

Right on cue, a ruby-throated Hummingbird zooms to the feeder outside the kitchen window. I can see it hovering, its wings a blur, just beyond my father's shoulder. It's not such a big coincidence. They feed about every three seconds. They're the only birds in the world with ADD.

"So this black-chin; there's only a few left?"

Dad shakes his head again. "It's not an endangered species. It's just that they summer in Texas, not Eastern Canada. This little fellow is thousands of kilometres from home."

He rubs his hands together. It's as if his whole day just took on a brighter hue. Then he glances hopefully my way.

"Want to come?"

I groan inside. When I was little, I enjoyed clambering around in other people's hedges to spy on wrens and warblers, but the thrill has gone.

Oh, but the look on his face. I check my watch. It's only ten. And after all, I want to do my part towards bringing about world peace, if only in the Whiticar family. "Okay," I say, a little slow on the uptake. "As long as we're back by dinner."

From the look on Dad's face, that's not an option.

"Ottawa?" I say, when he explains where this tiny Texas fugitive has been sighted. "That's like 400 kilometres away."

"Not quite Ottawa," he quickly adds. "Some little place in the country northwest of there. Bob is going to fax me a map. A place called Elphin."

I try to imagine what kind of a road map leads to somewhere called Elphin. "Can we put it off until next weekend?"

He explains that it's a very rare occurrence and I explain how getting a date is a very rare occurrence and he explains how there'll be plenty of dates down the road and I explain that there'll be plenty of birds down the road and then he's about to play his next card but he stops mid sentence, takes a deep breath and says he understands.

That's something else he does a lot lately. We hardly ever get up a good head of steam on an argument, any more, before he bales. I see a flicker of tension along his jaw and realize how much this understanding costs.

Then the phone rings again. Good, I think. It's Bob to say the sighting was a hoax. But the joke's on me. It's Delia and the date is off.

†¤†¤†

So there we are, Dad and I are speeding along old

Highway Seven northbound to adventure! Bob cancelled. Maybe he suddenly remembered he had a life. It's all rough and tumble up here. Bush as far as the eye can see. Rock and pine and wetland. There is a lake around every curve of the highway. Some are little more that beaver-dammed ponds littered with the grey trunks of dying trees. I find the Tragically Hip on the radio, then lose them again. Even radio waves get lost in these endless woods.

This is the fringe of the Canadian Shield, the oldest mountain range in the world but worn down to low slung hills. I wonder what that little hummingbird thought when he landed here. This isn't Texas anymore, Toto.

Dad smokes. He never used to. It's a nervous habit and being alone with me in the car seems to make him nervous. He cranks open his window and hangs half his torso outside in an attempt to save me from second-hand smoke. But that doesn't save me from the second-hand worry. I remember Mom's word. *Intimidé*. I intimidate him. And I don't know why.

He closes the window and natters about faculty politics at the university where he teaches math. Now that we only see each other every other week he saves this stuff up. I try to be interested but it's pretty dull and it never stops. Then suddenly it does.

Which is how I must have missed the signpost, I

realize later.

Dad stops talking. I see his hands tighten on the wheel. There is panic in his eyes. I'm afraid he's having a stroke.

"Are you okay?"

"I'm fine," he says too quickly, training his eyes on the road. He looks as if he's going to say more and I wait. That's how I must have missed the sign. Too busy observing Dad.

You've heard of the back of beyond? Elphin is beyond that. It's like a trip back in time. We're climbing up into the Lanark Highlands and I keep expecting to see some Ojibwa hunter standing on the shoulder staring at the cracked and pitted pavement of County Road 36 wondering how it got there. So it is all the more astounding to come upon so many cars after kilometres of nothing. Twenty-three vehicles I count pulled well off onto the verge under a canopy of maples alive with summer breezes.

In a clearing is a tidy little log house, obviously owned by the three bears. This is the object of our pilgrimage? No. Something buzzing around that neat little house. Something the size of a sugar cube, a sugar cube with attitude. There are license plates from as far away as Québec, New York and Vermont. There's even a van from a TV station.

Dad gathers his camera equipment together and we head off to join the eager throng. Except that Dad sees a candy wrapper and has to stop to pick it up. He pockets it. He has this thing about litter.

†††††

The birders wait patiently by the roadside until they are invited, in small clutches, to see THE BIRD. Dad bides his time, chatting with fellow birders and occasionally stooping to swoop up a gum wrapper.

The three bears turn out to be three nice hippies: Papa Hippy with a ponytail, Momma Hippy with a longer ponytail and Baby Hippy with the longest ponytail of all. They seem to enjoy the company. Mamma Hippy has baked brownies and Baby Hippy shows everyone his tree fort.

Black-chin, clearly, does *not* enjoy the company. He's in a foul mood. But then, in my limited experience, hummingbirds are always in a foul mood. You'd be in a foul mood if waking up in the morning was enough to kill you. It's true! Hummingbirds sometimes have heart attacks just waking up.

The little heart-attack-in-training darts around, dive-bombing the birders and dive-bombing the local ruby-throats as well. The weird thing is, it takes me a long time to distinguish this accidental tourist from the locals. I was hoping for something neon yellow with racing stripes. But black-chin looks just like the ruby-throats as far as I can tell: long beak, bad temper. In a reverent whisper, Dad points out the purple band around the stranger's throat.

For a purple band we have driven 317 kilometres?

Finally, our turn is up and we head back out towards the road.

Goldilocks is waiting.

She's in red high heels. She's got a microphone in hand, a cameraman on a chain, and from twenty metres away you can see that she's singled Dad out from the herd. He immediately lights up another cigarette.

I observe him through the smoke. He looks calm enough. No one else would know he was nervous. And I am, too, because I can't help noticing how good-looking he is. It's not supposed to matter how your father looks. But I see Goldilocks fuss with her hair, and it makes me jumpy.

"You don't have to talk to her," I whisper.

"That would be rude," he whispers back. He takes one last long drag on his cigarette and bravely smiles for the camera.

"Ornery little cuss, isn't he?" says Goldilocks, flashing a hundred-watt smile. There are introductions all around but Goldilocks only has eyes for Dad. "The bird attacked my cameraman," she says. "And he only weighs three grams."

Dad grins, pleasantly. "He looks to me as if he

weighs closer to ninety kilos."

"Oh, that is so funny," squeals Goldilocks. "Did you catch that, Ray?"

The cameraman holds up his hand to indicate he's rolling, and Goldilocks puts on her TV face.

"I'm talking to Terry Whiticar who drove all the way up here from Toronto with his son to witness this rare event. What do you think brought this little fellah our way, Terry?" she asks.

Dad shrugs. "Maybe someone in Houston sneezed," he says.

Goldilocks is in raptures. She's getting good tape. I figure this must be a big step up from reading the weather.

"Some people say he might have lost his sense of direction," she says. "Others say he got caught up in a trade wind. What's your take, Terry?"

Dad looks back across the lawn to where the latest gaggle of birders is gathered in silent awe. His face becomes thoughtful. "Maybe it wasn't an accident," he says.

Goldilocks looks surprised. "Really?"

Dad turns to her and his face is serious, almost pained. "Maybe things were just so bad back home, he had to get away."

And that's when his pants go up in flames.

Well, not flames, exactly, but they sure as heck are on

fire. Remember the cigarette? Dad slipped the butt into his pocket along with all the other trash. He just didn't quite put the butt out first. Suddenly he is dancing around hitting himself and I'm running after him hitting him, too. All I can think is that I've got to put Dad out!

Sure enough, Mr black-chin gets in on the act, chasing us, his wings making this low whirring whistle over our heads, until Papa Hippy solves everything with a bucketful of water. It's well water from the cold clear depths of the oldest mountains in the world.

♦♦♦♦♦

Ray gets the whole song and dance on tape. Goldilocks takes Dad's address so she can send him a copy. Right.

"That was so stupid," I shout, when we're back in the car. "You could have seriously hurt yourself." Dad turns the car around and we head back down to the world.

"I'm sorry," he says.

"I don't *want* you to be sorry," I shout. "I don't *want* you to understand. I don't *want* you to be so polite that you go up in flames."

There's silence for about three-tenths of a kilometre. He reaches for his cigarettes then changes his mind. He clears his throat.

"I'm sorry for apologizing," he says.

It's a joke. I *know* it's a joke, but for some reason I bellow at him to shut up and then, before I know what's hit me, I'm crying. It's totally absurd. I sob and sniffle and basically dissolve right there on the passenger's seat.

"*Where's Michel?" Mom asks. "Oh, he dissolved, sorry.*"

Dad is smart enough not to say anything. It's not about the fire. It's about everything. Anyway, it is through a veil of stale tears that I see the road sign. The one I missed on the way up.

"Oompah," I say, like a tuba.

Dad says nothing.

I turn as we pass the sign and read it out loud. "Turn Right for Oompah. Why does that ring a bell?"

Still nothing. But I notice Dad's hands tighten on the wheel. He's wearing pants he borrowed from Papa Hippy. Faded yellow jeans with crazy patches on them. His face looks kind of yellow too. We're driving into the sunset.

"It's Ompah," he says at last. "To rhyme with stomp."

I sniff and wipe my wet face. "You mean to rhyme with stompa," I correct him.

His smile is grim. He shakes his head as if he's trying to jiggle something loose in his skull. Then all of a sudden he slows down the car.

"Dad?"

No answer. We just roll to a stop. My window's down and the evening air is filled with cricket song and the screech of blue jays.

"The Ompah Stomp," he says. "The big end of summer hoedown."

Then I remember. "Ompah. Of course! That's where you grew up."

He shakes his head. "The road to Ompah," he says, as if there is an important difference. He seems lost in thought. I sit back, feeling empty and exhausted.

I notice that we've pulled to a stop right at the intersection of Highway 509, the road to Ompah. There's a big homemade sign at the intersection, "Blue Skies," it reads, with an arrow pointing north.

"So that's where those blue skies got to," I say.

I look at Dad. He's ticking. It's his brain, I think, ticking like a time bomb. Then I notice it's just his fingernail on the steering wheel. His eyes look as if he's watching a horror movie and it's come to the scene with the knife and the bathtub. I want to reach out and touch him but I resist the urge. I don't want him to go off.

He must be remembering his parents. They died years and years ago, as far as I know. There's no pictures, no cards. I don't think he was a happy kid. Watching him now, he doesn't *look* like a happy kid.

He clears his throat. "*Archilocus alexandri*," he says, so quietly I can hardly hear him. The hill gets a little older, erodes just a little more before he speaks again. "Maybe that bird was sent to me," he says.

Now I'm really worried. Can a fire in your pants actually fry your brain? But he chuckles — seems to guess what I'm thinking.

"Sorry," he says. "I'm not making much sense."

I shrug. "Yeah, well, join the club."

It turns out, he's still thinking about the black-chin. "Nothing else would have brought me up this way," he says. "I don't know why I've avoided it so long." He looks at me squarely. "Do you mind if we pay a little visit?" he asks.

I groan, partly from hunger and partly from apprehension, but I keep it to myself.

♦ ♦ ♦ ♦ ♦

There's another homemade sign a little farther up the road. "You're almost there!" it says. Blue Skies, I guess. Is that where we're going? Looking at Dad's bleak expression I don't think so.

Then suddenly he puts on his indicator light, slows down and pulls off 509 onto a dirt driveway. I catch sight of the name on the battered black mailbox. The letters are cracked and peeling but the ghost of them remains. "Whiticar," it says.

The driveway climbs through stunted trees and moss-covered granite glowing pink in the setting sun. The bush closes in around us. Tall weeds brush the sides of the car. Then we come to a clearing, littered with cannibalized cars and scrawny chickens that flutter out of our path as we come to a stop in a cloud of our own dust. Before us sits a rambling, tarpaper shack. There's a porch with a bowed and rusted tin roof held up by arthritic log posts. A man is standing in the shadows on the stoop. He steps out into the sunlight. His shadow is a lot longer than he is. He's wearing filthy grey overalls with the bib down and a T-shirt stained yellow around the armholes. He comes down the steps. He's got a farmer's tan; his lower arms look oven-roasted, his upper arms are as white as bone. He's got a grizzled grey beard, a balding head and there's a scowl brewing on his face. I glance nervously at Dad for some clue. An uncle? A second cousin three hundred times removed? Dad is staring straight ahead at the unfriendly looking geezer, as if he's in a trance.

This other Whiticar is making his way towards us, kicking at chickens that cross his path. Dad opens the door and steps out and quickly I do the same. We slam our doors shut simultaneously, as if we're Starsky and Hutch arriving on the scene of the crime but in a white and timid-looking Honda.

Mr Chicken-Kicker may be short but he's as solid as a drum. His arms and rounded shoulders look strong, despite his age. He's got a long rod in his hand. Some part of a tractor, I guess: oily and rusty, with a chain at the end. He stops, looks Dad up and down, his scornful eyes resting on the faded yellow hippy jeans.

"Does this look like a music festival?" he says. He sounds like he just ate a bucketful of gravel. "It's another mile to Blue Skies," he adds. Dad doesn't answer. "Are ya deaf?" the old man shouts. "Or just stoned?" He has reached the front of our car now and he raises his rod as if he's going to strike the grill.

"How about I put your lights out," he shouts. "Will that wake ya up?"

He brings his improvised weapon down hard on the ground. I gasp and a smirk lights up his face. And then it dawns on him who he's talking to and it dawns on me at the same instance, who this swamp creature must be. My father is slim and tall but the flecks of grey in his black hair is the same as the grey of this man's beard. My father will one day grow bald in the same way as this man. And, looking at my father now, I see an exact reflection of the other's anger. He is my grandfather and he is anything but dead.

"Well, well," he says. "What brings you here?"

"I was in the neighbourhood."

Grandfather cackles. With the salutations out of the way, he turns his attention to me. "This yours?" he asks, as if I were a used car.

"This is Michel, my son," says Dad. His voice is brittle.

The old man assesses me the way a butcher might weigh up a side of lamb. "He looks soft," he says. He makes the word sound like the first symptom of a terminal disease. "Is that why you gave him a girl's name?"

"He's a good boy," says my father. "A wonderful boy. But I wouldn't expect you to recognize that."

Old Mr Whiticar doesn't favour his son with so much as a glance. His eyes are trained on me and filled with mischief. "Hear the way he talks to his old dad?" he says. "Nice, eh?"

I don't answer. I feel as if I've fallen down a rabbit hole. The Mad Hatter is moving now, coming around to my side of the car.

"He bad-mouth me a lot, kid?"

Even if I could speak, the words would never make it to the top of this pit I'm in. He leans against the car.

"You're a meek little son of a bitch," he says. "Does he beat ya?"

I look at Dad. I want him to do something – to at least say something but his mouth is clamped shut. I see that flicker of a pulse along his jaw, like a worm under the skin. I turn to his father and shake my head.

"He hit me once," says the old man rubbing his belly. "Can you believe it?" He sneers. "He only tried it once."

He slides his oil-stained hand along the car as he comes towards me. I back up – can't help it – until my hand is resting on the door handle. He smiles a bully's smile of satisfaction. And it's like a toehold for me, somehow; at the very bottom of my pit I start to climb.

The man sidles up closer, glancing sideways to assess how this is going over with Dad. Dad observes, nothing more. Now, Grandfather Whiticar is close enough to smell the sourness of him. At close quarters I see the bitterness in his pale grey eyes. "I'd watch him, if I were you," he says in a stage whisper. He indicates my father with a wag of his head. "Got a temper on him like a wild turkey."

I clear my throat. "I can see where he gets it from."

Grandfather's amused face darkens. "What's that, boy?"

I let go of the door handle and step up to him. "If my father has a temper, I can see why."

The old man rubs his bearded chin. He looks hard at me. "Your dad there, he got real insolent round about your age." His face is right up close to mine, except he's shorter, and he has to look up. "Don't pay to be rude to me, boy," he says poking himself in the chest.

I nod. "I think I understand."

"Good, good," he says, backing off a step, as if I've passed a test. And now he looks across the car towards my father. "Big shot over there never did. Thought he was something special. Thought the sun shone out of his butt."

I interrupt him. "I meant I think I understand

why my father never talked about you."

"He didn't?"

"Never."

"Why?"

"Because you aren't worth talking about."

I see his hand jerk – the one holding the weapon – but I'm quicker than he is and plant my foot on the chain. The whole rusty thing leaps from his hand and clatters to the ground.

"Little bastard," he says. And he steps towards me with his meaty hand raised. Dad shouts and stops the old man in his tracks.

"Michel!"

He sounds so angrily.

"Apologize to your grandfather," he demands.

I can't believe it. I turn towards him – towards my father. He's staring at me intently across the hood of the car and there is rage in his eyes.

"Are you crazy?"

He nods. "You bet I am!" he shouts. And he looks it, too. His eyes are on fire. "Do as I tell you, ya hear?"

My jaw drops. Did he really say "Ya hear?" I turn to the old man. His jaw has dropped. We're on the jaw dropping side of the car. Dad, on the other hand – his jaw is set. Firm.

Fine. Two can play at this game. Now I'm angry. Furious.

"I am not going to—"

"Oh, yes you are!" Dad fires back at me before I can even finish. His voice is huge. He brings his fist down hard on the roof of the car. And maybe that's what wakes me up. I'm just about to mount the attack when suddenly I understand.

A whole tumble of things makes sense all at once. His rage is not for me. And there is more in his eyes than rage − a lot more. There is a furious spark of defiance and a wicked glint of humour. *I get it.* I get it all in one atom-splitting instant. And I know *exactly* what I have to do, only I'm not sure I can pull it off. I turn to face my aggressor. I try to talk but I have to clear my throat first. I try again.

"I'm sorry, Granddad," I say, as humbly and submissively as I can muster. "I didn't mean to be impolite."

It's amazing. It works like a charm. It is a charm, because when I glance quickly at my father he looks as if he's been released from a spell. It's as if my apology has slammed a door in the old man's face. He can't get at my father any more.

When we turn the car around to go he's still standing in the same place, still rubbing the wrist of his right arm. But in my last glimpse of him in the side view mirror, he looks old. As if anger was all that was holding him together. All his beautiful wickedness.

As the summer evening settled around the car, Dad tells me of the time he punched his father. The old man had been terrorizing Grandma and Dad couldn't take it any longer. He hit him and knocked him down. Then he left and never came home again. He was thirteen, like me. He wrote to his mother, worried about her. She wrote back and told him that she could look after herself but she could not look after him, so it was just as well he was gone.

Silence descends but a companionable silence. Dad never once reaches for his smokes. It's a long time before he talks again.

"When we started fighting, it frightened me," he says.

"I bet it did. He's so strong."

"I mean when *you and I* started fighting," says my father.

I turn to look at him. "Fighting? Us?"

"Arguing," he says. "You know. Questioning me. Expressing your own opinion. Suddenly, everything I said wasn't automatically right any more. It caught me off guard. Outraged me. And my outrage frightened me. I was afraid I was becoming him. And I couldn't let that happen."

I stared out through my own reflection at the night. It was all beginning to make some kind of sense.

I looked back at Dad. "You *are* allowed to disagree with me, Dad," I say to him. "Just as long as you realize that I'm *always* right, we'll get along just fine."

His face breaks into a moonlit smile. "I understand," he says. But when I look at him a little later on, he's not smiling any more. He's thinking about his father, I can tell. Something is over, maybe. The spell may be broken. But when things get broken there are always those bits and pieces of whatever it was lying around. Dad looks as if he's looking at all those bits and pieces wondering what happened.

👥👥👥👥👥

He wakes me as we fly down the Don Valley Expressway. He's found an Oldies station playing *Wouldn't It Be Nice* by the Beach Boys.

"I was thinking we should get a pizza," he says. "Maybe drop by your mom's place. You think she'd be up for a party?"

I rub the sleep out of my eyes and check the clock. "At 2.00 a.m.?"

He nods enthusiastically. "I'm talking about a really big pizza, Michel. With banana peppers and anchovies and both kinds of olives. What do you say?"

I nod. Apart from the anchovies, it sounds great. We can argue about that at the pizzeria. I look ahead down the empty freeway. It won't be dawn for hours yet, but I think I can almost see the light.

# Superdad

## FRANCIS MCCRICKARD

I was angry, as angry as I'd ever been with Dad. He shouldn't have tried to talk to Amy. He should have just said hello and disappeared to wherever he disappears to regularly these days; gone on one of his mystery outings.

"Amy? Nice name. Anagram of *May*. You weren't born in that month, were you? Stephen's birthday's coming up soon; April. What do you think of all this snow? They say there's more to come... You at school with Stephen? Hope you don't distract him from his studies, ha, ha! Wouldn't take much to do that, mind you. Not that you're *not much*... You're... No, not at all... You're... You're... actually you're the first girl he's brought home... *Our* boy... Stephen Maley... growing up... his first girlfriend... If that's what you are? I mean, I don't... Want to see some photographs?"

That did it really. That was the final straw. Just a few weeks short of my thirteenth birthday, I realized I didn't like my dad and found him intensely embarrassing. I could stick him for short periods. On the couch at home, watching television, if he kept his mouth shut, didn't try to answer when quiz shows were on, didn't say that someone would never do whatever they'd just done on one of the soaps, didn't tell me yet again that boys should support their local football team when I was cheering for Man U, I could put up with him. It was all right as well when he showed me shortcuts on his computer or brought me some new games software, as long as he just did whatever he needed to do and didn't hang around my room trying some awkward father-son bonding. Up with that I could not put, as *he* might cringe-inducingly say.

It hadn't always been like that.

My favourite photograph, one Dad didn't show Amy, was taken when I was six. It's blu-tacked to one of my bedroom walls. Dad had woken me early and told me that we were going into the wilderness to hunt. It was a clear, mid-October day with a loud whisper of winter cold in the air. I remember he wrapped me up tightly, first pulling a thick woollen jumper over my head, then lapping a long, bright red scarf around my neck and body, knotting it in the middle of my back, and topping that with my waterproof jacket. Our big busy estate was on the edge of town and short walks led us quickly to country lanes and quiet tidy villages. Although I was excited, I was still very tired and Dad carried me a lot of the way on his shoulders to a farm owned by family friends, James and Marie. There, in front of a huge wood fire, we breakfasted on chunks of bread still hot from the oven and smothered in butter and homemade blackcurrant jam. I wanted to take my coat and the scarf off, but Dad told me that we would be going soon.

"Can't hang around. Early morning's the best time. They're still sleepy. You can get up close, catch them unawares."

I thought I saw Marie smiling, but Dad kept telling me very seriously that what we were going to do was very dangerous:

"It's a jungle out there, son. Anything can happen."

I hung on every word Dad said. I had to follow instructions and do exactly what I was told. After breakfast, we had ventured into the "wilderness", a small orchard on the farm, and, staying upwind of our prey, "hunted" the large, dark red Spartan apples. Dad twisted a length of thick wire into a fork and inserted it into the top of a bamboo pole. This was my hunting spear and with it I jolted the apple stalks until the fruit fell. Dad stood underneath with a large net to stop them hitting the ground.

"If they hit the ground, they could open up and their tentacles will come out. They're like octopuses.

Octopuses are their cousins. Octopuses used to live up trees but the leaves, chestnut leaves especially, gave them a rash and that's why they went to the sea. They all went on a bus, not a double-decker because it's hard to climb stairs with eight tentacles. So don't let them hit the ground. If you do, they'll wrap their tentacles around you and take you back to their planet, Planet Ripe. And if they get you to Planet Ripe, you have to clean their houses each day and all they give you to eat is worms. Sometimes, they dip the worms in chocolate, but it isn't very nice chocolate and you wouldn't like it, Stephen, honestly."

Dad took four big strides. "Their tentacles are really long, as long as that, and they go around you tighter than your scarf."

My head was tilted upwards for so long spotting the apples, dense and black against the jigsaw blue of the sky, that it hurt a little when I righted it. Sometimes, my jolt with the pole would send the fruit arcing away from us and Dad had to run and sometimes dive to stop it falling to the earth. Each time, when he caught them, he'd fall on top of the net, wrestle with the apple and pretend to beat it until it stopped resisting. Dad caught all the apples I knocked down and they never got him with their tentacles.

It was great; a magical morning. I loved it all. James came to the orchard with a camera and a special hat. It was a pith-helmet, one of those worn by hunters in Africa years ago. It was far too big for my head, but James put it on me and I stood alongside Dad with the pole over my shoulder like a rifle and our "kill", a fat sack of the dark crunchy apples, on the ground in front of us. We posed looking serious and proud while James took the photograph. In it, I'm looking up at my dad from under the big helmet.

"You're a great hunter, Stephen," Dad had told me. "I'm very proud of you."

Drizar Farm was one of my favourite places. Three other visits during that same year convinced me that my dad was a superhero and perhaps even God. On the first of those visits, I watched Dad and James stack bales of hay in one of the two big barns; stack them as neatly as Lego blocks until they almost reached the roof. I sat most of the afternoon in the barn entrance with Gem, the sheepdog, drinking lemonade that Marie had made and watching the two men work. Dad was like a powerful machine, bending, spearing, lifting, his back bow-taut, tossing, then bending, spearing, lifting... As the stack rose, the two men made steps of bales so that they could lift and pile the rows higher and higher, and as the thick, warm atmosphere wreathed me and I became mesmerized by the steady, repeated choreography, I began to believe that my dad might be a superhero, and I fell asleep, my head on the patient dog's side.

The shed came next. Dad helped James rebuild a stone shed. Once again, I played with Gem and watched my father work for most of a hot July afternoon. He had never looked so big and powerful as when he lifted carefully the heavy stones and lowered them on to the slubber of mortar and it was the placing of the huge lintel stone, nearly one-and-a-half metres long and almost half a metre wide, that told me my dad had super powers.

The two men lifted the great stone together. James was the bigger man, but as the weight reached shoulder height, it became too much for him. His arms shook with the strain; he faltered, and it looked for a moment as if he was going to drop the stone while Dad lifted his end high until one corner rested on stone above the door space and he could help his friend. He steadied the lintel at the side and placed his other hand under the stone at James' end. That hand held my gaze: a hydraulic jack of human muscle pumping upwards, straight, unerring, unwavering, and, for a second, I was sure, lifting the stone right out of James' grasp, until that end too found its niche. It was a hand that could hold up the world; it was the hand of God that I had seen in a Reception Class book. I lay on my back and watched scraps of cloud turn into great leaden fists that hurled javelins of rain at us. My dad had done that as well, I was sure.

And finally, at the farm again, mending a trailer, Dad had worn what could only be described as a superhero's helmet that covered his head and shoulders. Standing well back behind him, I saw an intense jet of flame come from his eyes and melt metal. What more proof was needed? My father was a superhero. When he walked alongside me, the man was huge and when he took my hand, that grip, I was sure, contained the power to uproot trees, demolish and rebuild houses in an instant and even hurl small planets through the universe.

We stopped going to the farm: "A shame… James wasn't old… wonder if they'll ever find a cure… probably build a new estate there". In the years that immediately followed, I continued to believe that my father was a superhero, but I no longer witnessed wonderful, superhuman feats performed by him. Doubts tiptoed into my mind. I looked for ways to banish them. When I was about eight, strong winds shifted some slates and Dad went on the roof to fasten them back in place. This was a great opportunity. If he was a superhero, he would have no problem getting off the roof without the ladder. I used a hammer to remove the wedge Dad had placed at the bottom and then I pushed the ladder sideways.

It was heavier than I thought but slowly it shifted until the top slithered along the guttering and fell to the ground. Before it collapsed, I ran into the front doorway and waited there for Dad to glide down from the roof or use super-willpower to make the ladder erect itself exactly where it had been. After five minutes, the front door opened behind me and Dad came out of the house:

"You all right, Stephen? Good job the skylight was open."

Barnabas, the neighbour's cat, provided the next test. Dad had been turning some soil in the border round our small front lawn and I had been sitting on the front step playing with toy cars. The driver of the van was looking for a house number and wasn't driving fast. Something spooked Barnabas and he raced out of next door's bushes into the road. Dad wasn't looking at the road and couldn't have seen Barnabas from where he was working, but superheroes have extra senses for those times, haven't they? They can *see* without looking directly at whatever it is; they *feel* fear and anxiety and respond to them. Dad didn't move. There was a slight screech of rubber as the driver braked. I shouted, "Dad!" at the same time. Dad did move then. He put the garden fork through his shoe and broke one of his toes. Barnabas was killed.

I thought a lot about what had happened and came up with an interesting theory. As a superhero, my dad could have saved Barnabas but he didn't because superheroes are not allowed to go about advertising themselves and fixing everything. They have been given special powers and part of the deal is that they have to use them anonymously and only for serious disasters that are threatening. Unless you are on superhero duty, you acted as if there was nothing at all special about you. You advertised yourself as ordinary, dull. You acted like my dad acted! That was the code you had to follow. It made sense. If you paraded around as a superhero all the time, you would upset a necessary balance in the world. Just think about it. People would never leave you alone. With every problem that came their way, big or little, they'd insist on the help of the superheroes. I could see my seventeen-year-old cousin, Sarah, breaking a nail and calling on Superdad to reverse time, or Mum never cooking again because Dad microwaved everything with his eyes, or me making Dad blow an opposition striker's goal-bound shot off course. Nobody would do anything for themselves. The world would be too easy. Another problem would be that people would go out of business because the superheroes were on the job. Your home is demolished in a storm? Normally, architects, builders, plumbers, electricians, carpenters would be queuing up to make you a new home but if Superman is in the Yellow Pages, you call him up and he reassembles the old one in a second and doesn't charge you a thing. Everyone would be bothering them. They'd be rescuing spooked cats every day. It wouldn't be right and would distract them from important work such as patching holes in bursting dams, rounding up gangsters who are threatening to wipe out a city with nerve gas or lassoing asteroids that are on a collision course with earth. They have to save themselves for the big stuff and that's why they try to remain anonymous. They don't even tell their family or their best friends.

I could understand why Dad had not rescued Barnabas. You didn't reveal your true identity for the sake of a ten-year-old cat.

In spite of this theory my doubts increased, and an argument and a coffee cup helped them grow. Usually, whenever my parents argued, they used special radar to keep their quarrels on a flight path above mine and so they seldom troubled me directly. However, late on a sticky July evening, they were not so discreet. I heard raised voices and lifted my head from my pillow to hear better.

My mother: "… you could have finished it…"

A breeze from the window dried the sweat on

my cheek.

My father: "… can't expect… I'm not Superman."

He admitted it.

The following morning at the breakfast table, they were very quiet and unsmiling. I watched my dad clenching a cup of coffee between his big hands. The cup would shatter any minute, I thought, and she would realize who she had married. Then I remembered the code of secrecy that superheroes have to maintain. If Mum knew, she wouldn't be able to keep it from the other mums at school or her workmates at the bank. She'd tell her mum and her hairdresser and then everyone would know and that wouldn't be right. They'd all be queuing up outside our door to have their DIY done for nothing. Nevertheless, on that July morning, I wanted the coffee cup to shatter; I wanted him to prove he had superpowers. The cup didn't break.

I stopped believing the code-theory and slowly started to see Dad in a different way. As I grew nine, ten, eleven, my dad shrank. As my world became bigger – soccer; computer games, mobile, clothes; rock music, girls – my dad's became smaller. I began to realize that he was like other dads – except for Joe Naylor's who drove rally cars – and was *ordinary* and dull, embarrassingly dull *all of the time*. I really wanted to think otherwise, but it was no use. He was *something* in computers and sat at a desk all day; he listened to Radio 4; he read a lot of history; didn't go to the cinema and didn't play a sport of any kind. He did turn out for the *Dad's versus Lads* soccer game in my last week at primary school but it had been embarrassing. He'd worn heavy, navy coloured shorts that reached over his knees and a borrowed sweatshirt that read: THE ENFORCER. The other dads were kitted in the latest gear and a couple of them played for local amateur clubs. My dad scored two own goals and injured another dad by falling on him heavily. I tried to convince my friends that he had been having a laugh and could play really well if he wanted to, but no one believed me.

Dad's passion for fashion continued off the football pitch. He hardly ever bought anything new and I was sure that, with the exception of bargains from the Premier Factory Shop such as the ever-present, green/purple, *Windy Ridge* fleece, he got his clothes by picking through bags of throwouts at the back of the Oxfam charity shop. For example, there was the shapeless, dark brown, woollen cardigan, the brown, *Hot Diggity* comfort fit jeans with the slack crotch, and the worn, holed, white, plastic *Supremo* trainers ("Last a lifetime, these will").

I hated parents' evenings at school. Dad dressed up for those.

*Clothes maketh the man.* I knew that wasn't true. A bigger problem was that dad's body didn't do much to *maketh* him either. It was like a bulging cocktail sausage. His head was a smaller version of the same shape, a stubby cube with rounded corners. And on top, although he wasn't all that old, his sandy hair was sparse, wispy. The only place hair seemed to grow well was in his nose and this supergrowth played its part in changing the way I thought about the man who was my father. I had been sitting on the floor between his legs watching television one evening. In the adverts, I'd thrown my head back at the same time as Dad leant forwards and I had the best view I could possibly have up his nostrils. What I saw and what happened horrified me. Even though I heard the programme coming back on again, I couldn't take my eyes off those caverns of darkness. On a snow-covered landscape, they were twin tunnels that led to the mountain lair of an evil monster. The hair was dense and wiry like the stuff doormats are made of. It was so thick that I wondered if air ever got up there. I was thinking that our doormat could be made of Dad's nose hair when suddenly, without any warning, he sneezed and I found out there was a passage through that dense jungle.

It was a superhuman sneeze. "Sorry, son, sorry," he kept repeating as he wiped my face with the nearest cloth to hand, a pair of his shapeless Y-fronts that were drying on a radiator, underpants he never wore over his trousers.

And so it all changed. Apart from when he gave me more pocket money or refused to let me go somewhere, Dad did get smaller. What I mean is that he became more and more unimportant in my life. At times, I remembered the farm and the happiness there but the doubts continued to grow stronger. The change was gradual but, long before I started wondering if any special plans were being made for my thirteenth birthday, I stopped believing Dad was any kind of a hero, never mind a superhero. In fact, I couldn't understand how I had ever thought such a thing could be true. I must have been a very *sad* kid.

Almost every Saturday and Sunday throughout the winter before my thirteenth birthday, Dad disappeared and spent three or four hours away from the house. Sometimes he went to wherever he went in the car; sometimes he walked. I was reluctant to show any interest in anything he did, but I did ask him once where he was going. He replied by tapping the side of his nose and saying nothing. When I asked my mother, she just shrugged her shoulders, smiled and said, "He's going out". I thought she looked a little sad when she said this. The only clue I had to go on was the spade I saw him carry on one of these outings.

These unexplained absences began to annoy me and my mind spun with possibilities. A ridiculous thought, a remnant of the childhood fantasies, crossed my mind. These disappearances could be superhero times when Dad was circumnavigating the earth plugging erupting volcanoes, deflecting thermo-nuclear devices into outer-space and generally averting huge disasters. The thought made me laugh and think again how stupid I'd been thinking all that stuff in the past. I understood the *real* world now. A drink problem: that's what it could be but there were never any telltale signs when Dad returned: no wobbles, slurred speech, anger or stinking clothes. Higher on my list of possibilities was the thought that he was seeing another woman. The idea sickened me. *Seeing*: it was funny the words people used to describe something so nasty. The spade? He was doing some gardening for her as well as *seeing* her.

HEROES OF TODAY: that's what was written on the whiteboard for our Tutor Group Study class. Form Tutor Barry Johnson blinked rapidly behind his large lens glasses.

"Hero," he said, followed by the strange noise that sounded like, "*Em…uurr*" and had gained him the nickname of the Third Wise Man. "Hero… *em…uurr…* is a much abused word." Myles Traynor was bent over with his head completely immersed in his schoolbag; Gemma Loughlin was reapplying a false nail; Neil Thirlwell was texting; Ralph Ormesby, strange boy, was pulling those faces he always did, as if testing to see how wide he could make his mouth and Stephen Maley was… Stephen Maley was… I was paying attention. Well, I looked like I was paying attention. I was staring at the Third Wise Man but thinking of my old obsession with superheroes and the great pile of comics at the bottom of my bedroom wardrobe. I wondered how much I could sell them for.

"I repeat… *em…muurr…* a much abused word. Define a hero for me."

"He's strong…"

"Always a man?"

"He or she is strong."

"Physically?"

"Yes, physically."

"Not necessarily. Heroes… *emm…uurr…* can be strong in many ways. Can anyone else help us here?"

"Mentally strong."

"Good. I have no doubt in my… *err…muurr…* mind that your idea of such a person involves violence, someone who engages in Arnold Schwarzenegger-type exploits…"

Several boys aimed imaginary weapons and made

different shooting and exploding noises and everyone laughed at Clive Higgins when he came out with a strange "Ha–ha, ha–ha, ha–ha" sound. Matthew Burns stood and karate kicked Lisa Webster's desk.

"But… *emm…uurr…* heroes can be gentle. I want you to come up with other ways in which people can be heroes. Get away from the stereotypes."

The class listed ways in which people could be heroes: someone who invented new medicines; someone who looks after their invalid mother or father; someone who has a disability but just gets on with it and doesn't moan. Julia Masterson had heard of a man who was badly injured in a climbing accident and has two artificial legs, but he does all kinds of things and still goes up mountains. Mark Compton said there was a woman who had terminal cancer but she was cycling from John O'Groats to Lands End to raise money for research into the disease. Sarah Fallon said she'd read something in a magazine about a young woman who had this disease that made your face all distorted. Some people called her Desperate Dan because she had a huge chin but she didn't want operations to change how she looked because her face was *her.* Myles Traynor had an aunt who was a nun and worked in a hospital somewhere in Africa where there was war.

"Someone who tries to save the environment," said Gemma Loughlin.

"Good, that's a good one. We're getting somewhere with this. You're... *emm...uurr...* telling me that a hero is someone who cares for others and for the planet. Recycling, conservation; maybe there's something we can do as a class project along those lines, something practical, something to do with the environment..."

I could try selling the magazines on *eBay*.

After Amy's visit, I decided I was going to follow Dad and find out exactly what he was up to during those unaccounted for times on Saturdays and Sundays. Where did he go? What did he do? Why all the secrecy? I was curious and, to be honest, I wanted to get my own back on my thick insensitive father, especially for *anagram of May, first girlfriend* and the photographs. I wanted to find a club to beat him and blackmail him with whenever I felt like it: "If you don't let me, I'll tell Mum what you're up to."

Dad left on foot in the snow. I counted to fifty as I put my Geography field trip boots on and followed him. "Amy's!" I shouted through to Mum when she asked me where I was off to. "Back for tea!"

The petrol garage was at the edge of our estate. I knew Dad was heading for Drizar Farm when I saw him cross the garage forecourt, stepping around piles of dirty slushy snow, and turn right on to Briar Road.

When I reached that junction, I wondered seriously if I should go on. Did I really want to know what my dad was up to? Did I want the few remaining scraps of respect for my father to be pulled from me? My head felt strangely light as if air had been pumped into it and it wanted to separate from the rest of me. For a moment, I thought I was going to be sick and stepped off the pavement on to the dirty snow that covered the grass verge. What was this all about? Where was my father going? He could be... he could be... More horrible possibilities – gory ones - rushed into my mind. You heard about ordinary people; dull people like my dad who nobody suspected until bits of someone he'd chopped up were found on a rubbish tip. I remembered the spade. My dad didn't use the rubbish tips; he buried the bits out at Drizar Farm. I bent over slightly and took deep breaths but, when a car slowed down as it approached me, I stood upright again and walked briskly on in the direction Dad had gone.

Two hundred metres along Briar Road, another right turn set me on to a narrower road and half a mile along that was the entrance to the farm. The buildings were derelict now. Several of the windows were broken and slates were missing from the house. The snow here was undisturbed apart from my father's obvious tracks and other, smaller, indeterminate impressions. A jaundiced grey sky brooded over the roof of the farmhouse, a sign of more snow on the way.

I followed Dad's tracks through the old orchard and a collapsed gate into a narrow, hedged lane that I had no memory of. Slowly, carefully, I tried to place my steps in the imprints ahead of me. I didn't want Dad to know he had been followed. Although there was only a shoe size difference (me a 7, Dad an 8), Dad's stride was longer and I had to hop slightly to do this. The lane dipped steadily until it ran alongside a small wood. A stream with lacework of ice at the edges ran through the wood and across the lane. I was excited and breathed noisily in the cold air. The footprints led into the wood. Why had Dad gone into a wood with a spade? It had to be graves, shallow graves; they were always *shallow* graves. How many times had Dad come to this wood? There could be dozens of *shallow* graves.

I waited a few moments to calm myself and then stepped from the lane and over a stile to follow the footprints along the bank of the stream through the wood. I moved slowly, as silently as possible among the trees; like a hunter, I thought, and remembered the apples, that magical time with my father in the "wilderness". "You're a great hunter, Stephen. I'm very proud of you."

Every twenty metres or so, I froze to look and listen, and at those times became aware of the stillness and silence and had a strange feeling that the earth at that place had been waiting for me.

I was wondering how much further I would have to walk before my father's secret was revealed when I heard hammering. I darted behind a tree. My heart raced again. The hammering stopped, started, stopped. I tried to breathe slowly and quietly and, as I composed myself, I realized with a gasp that I wasn't the only one alarmed by the sound. Barely five metres from me on my right stood a young deer. It turned its head calmly from the direction of the noise and for a moment, looked straight at me. Hardly knowing what I was doing, I stepped forwards and reached out a hand to its russet side but the creature backed off, turned, its tail a white flame, and bounded away at an unhurried, self-possessed pace, lifting its legs high to be free of the crusted snow. I walked forwards another two paces and was sure I could still feel heat claiming the air where the deer had stood. Large snowflakes started to fall densely, gently through the branches above me.

When I reached the end of the wood, my first thought was that I was looking at tall, thin grave markers, *shallow* grave markers, but there were too many of them, row upon row of green tubes standing upright. They were like an army before the battle starts. They filled the lengthy, gently sloping bank on my side of the stream until it reached a boundary hedge and moorland a hundred metres along. Only a few speared out of the opposite bank but the snow was disturbed around them and more tubes and other materials lay on the ground. There was movement to my left on that bank and Dad emerged from the trunk of a huge oak tree at the edge of the wood! I stepped back into the trees until I was hidden but could watch what Dad was doing.

He carried a spade and a plastic sack (the bits of bodies) to the plot of disturbed snow. There, he started to dig, thrusting the spade through the crust of snow into the earth once, twice. His slight groans carried on the still air to me. After digging, he knelt down, lifted the flap of turf he had freed under the snow, took something – I couldn't quite see – from the sack and pushed it into the hole. He patted the earth back down and when he stood, made sure it was firm with his heel. Taking a heavy-headed hammer, he then drove a stake into the earth alongside. One of those tubes came next. He lowered it carefully down the side of the stake and fastened it to the stake with plastic ties.

I must have watched for about twenty minutes while Dad repeated this ritual half-a-dozen times.

There was nothing sinister about the weekend absences: no bodies, no women, no drink. He was planting trees, that's all, and, despite the cold, I was mesmerized and reassured again by the steadiness, the monotony of my father's movements as I had been almost seven years before when I'd watched Superdad pile bales of hay.

"Can I do one, Dad?"

"Stephen!" I'd startled him and he staggered and almost fell over some of the stakes lying in the snow. "What're you doing here?"

He didn't seem happy that I'd discovered his secret but he recovered quickly and forced a smile.

"Of course you can. We'll… we'll do some together."

"You sure?"

"Yes… yes, of course I am. It's great to have you here."

I still wasn't convinced that he thought that. I pointed to the planted bank. "You've done all this?"

Dad nodded.

"It's amazing. Why?"

Dad smiled more convincingly. "It's supposed to be a surprise for you. I wanted to have it all finished before you saw it."

"For me?"

"For you and, well, because we need to plant trees."

"Why now, in the snow?"

"Winter's the right time to plant."

Although the snow was falling thickly, we planted, staked and tubed twenty trees and, as light seeped from the sky, packed the tools, tubes, stakes into the cavernous hollow oak tree. As we did, Dad explained more.

"It's a present for your thirteenth birthday; your own wood. Your gran left a bit of money when she died and your mum and I decided to buy this land. The farm was being broken up and Marie made sure we got it for a reasonable price. I'd planned to plant a thousand trees by the time your birthday came around but I've underestimated how long that'd take me. As you can see, I've still most of this side of the stream to do."

I knew how we could fill that far bank with trees before my birthday and the Third Wise Man agreed with me, thought it was a wonderful idea.

"We'll do it, Stephen! We'll save the planet!"

On the five remaining Saturday mornings before my birthday, my tutor group, Dad and I planted four hundred and sixty-three ash, oak, cherry and hazel trees taking the total up to a thousand. My dad taught them how to plant carefully. He was happy and joked with them all. They liked him. They laughed, genuinely laughed, at his jokes.

"Your Dad's cool, Steve."

"Tree planting's great. I could do this all day."

"We're saving the planet."

"You're a hero, Mr Maley."

Things changed a lot with my visits to the wood. Throughout all the tree planting, I never felt angry or embarrassed because of Dad. It's hard to describe the new way I started to think about him. I suppose I have to use a word I've never used before and say that I began to *admire* him. I didn't tell anyone about how I felt.

Only Mum, Dad and I went to the plantation on my birthday. There were signs of spring everywhere. When we looked down the tubes, we saw the first green buds. The cherry trees were showing quickly; the oaks were slow and the ash even slower.

"But they're all right," Dad told me. "Slow and steady is good. It makes strong, hard wood."

The three of us stood at the highest point on the far bank of the stream. Mum linked Dad and he put his arm around my shoulders. Curlews made their long, liquid calls high above us.

"We're going to have a naming ceremony," said Dad.

"Has this place not got a name already?" I asked.

"The wood hasn't."

"What are you going to call it?"

"I've been on to the Ordnance Survey. I thought

you'd have guessed by now. This is *Stephen's Wood.*"

I sensed a slight movement to my right. A deer (the same deer?) stood at the edge of the old wood and stared at me.

# Later

SIMON CHESHIRE

G randma's brain was downloaded into the Family Archive android a few moments before she died. The rest of the family only got to hear about it when the Family Archive android came out of the house and told everyone what had happened.

Archive androids had been around for years – most families had one. Their databanks absorbed the minds of the aged and the sick, allowing loved ones to live on forever, as mental impulses, inside the android's body. Most Archive androids could store at least a dozen deceased relatives, and the posher models could store up to a hundred.

Twelve-year-old Sam was the first to notice what was going on. He'd been weeding the strawberry patch in the garden and wondering what Dad was up to at that exact moment. He looked around as the android stepped carefully out of the back door. It stepped carefully wherever it went, its long legs whirring slightly as it moved.

Then the android's smooth, grey outer shell

morphed in stages into the shape of Grandma, and so Sam knew that the real Grandma must now be dead. The android-as-Grandma gave him a cheery wave. He dropped his hoe, called over to Mum and hurried towards the house.

Everyone stopped their work on the garden for a while and gathered around the android-as-Grandma. It grinned at them all.

"Oh Grandmaaaa," sighed Mum. "Why didn't you say you were feeling poorly again?"

"Because I wasn't, dear," said the android-as-Grandma. "It just happened. There's no need to fuss. I'm perfectly fine, now, aren't I? My back pains have gone and everything. You know, I think I can help out with the garden for a while."

Everyone raised their hands in a 'no way' gesture. Mum and Auntie Jo and Uncle Bob, and cousin Sophie, and Sam.

"Don't be silly," said Auntie Jo.

"The Family Archive is too precious to let it work out in the garden, and you know it!" said Uncle Bob.

"Wish I was too precious too," mumbled Sophie under her breath. Only Sam heard her. Sophie was seventeen, and wanted to be out with Dad and the other work-hunters instead of looking after the crops.

"You're retired now Grandma," said Mum to the android. "You take it easy from now on."

The android-as-Grandma shrugged. Suddenly the android morphed again, this time into the appearance of old Grandad George. It had stored Grandad George twelve years ago, after his accident with the toaster.

"She never has done as she's told," said the android-as-Grandad-George in a gravelly voice, "not in all the time I've known her!"

They all laughed. The android-as-Grandad-George continued. "There's eight of us stored in this Archive now, and she's just going to have to get used to taking her turn along with me, and Old Nana and the rest of us. Daft old woman!"

They laughed again. The android switched back to Grandma.

"Anyone would think I could be stubborn or something!" said the android-as-Grandma.

Mum shook her head, giggling loudly. Sam put his hand on the android-as-Grandma's arm. "I'm glad you're okay," he said softly.

Grandma smiled down at him. "You're a good boy, Sam. Just like your father."

"Come on, let's go inside for a while," said Mum. "We could all do with a break."

"And don't be bothering with my old body," said Grandma. "I've dealt with it already myself. Straight into the recycling."

"Graaaandma," chorused the others.

Sam tailed behind for a moment, looking across the long wide garden at the mass of densely-grown and lovingly tended crops. There were potatoes and carrots, beans winding around tall bamboo poles, various fruits, and some asparagus and herbs for trading with neighbours. At the far end of the garden, the tall wind turbine stood completely still. The other turbines that Sam could see in all the neighbouring gardens were equally motionless. But the solar stacks, bolted to the roof of the house, soaked up the blistering sunlight. That's okay, then, thought Sam. We won't go short of power today.

The house was an ordinary one, in an ordinary street, in an ordinary town, in England Central B, in the August of 2064. Through the teleschool lessons on the Net, he'd done a project on his town through history. There were old 2D photos of his street static-clung to the wall of his room upstairs. One from 1922, when the houses had been built; one from 2002, when there was a big party in the street to celebrate the country's queen being around for fifty years (which was an idea he found quite odd); and one from 2015, when the first solar stacks had been installed. At that time, one big stack served the whole of his side of the street, because they'd been so expensive.

The street didn't look all that different now. Of

the trees that once sprouted from the pavements, the last had withered and died some years ago. These days, every house had its garden put to work, and its energy collecting systems, and of course there weren't any wasteful private cars around any more, but apart from that… the place didn't seem too different to how it looked in the photos.

That pleased Sam a lot. He enjoyed the thought that things could stay fixed like that.

Mum's face appeared out of the living room window. "Sam! I forgot to pull the shields! Could you do it before you come in?"

"Sure, Mum!" he called.

He flipped open a cover on the wall next to the tall wide conservatory, and turned the activation key inside. Right across the garden, thin membranes unfolded themselves on carbon fibre fingers. They covered the crops in a matter of seconds, letting through the sunlight, but cutting out some of the heat and the harmful rays that would otherwise destroy everyone's hard work.

It was almost lunchtime, and the heat was beginning to ripple from the concrete path which snaked away from the house. Sam adjusted his hat. Its wide brim was ideal for shading his eyes, but somehow it always felt heavy and cumbersome.

He sat on the step by the open conservatory

door. The garden was very quiet now that everyone was indoors. The neighbours were all indoors too, keeping out of the fiercest of the day's sun.

Sam loved moments like this. When it was utterly peaceful, and the only sound was the chirruping of the desert crickets in the undergrowth. It was in moments like this that he thought about Dad.

Sam couldn't wait to grow up. And be like Dad.

Dad had only been away for a couple of days, so far, this time. He was part of a work-hunting band, along with Uncle Matt, Auntie Susanna, and Jeff and Caroline who lived a couple of doors down.

Sam had studied basic economics, of course, through the teleschool, so he understood that being a work-hunter could be difficult, even dangerous. But even so, it seemed like a wonderful life. Glamorous and exciting. He'd read books about adventures on the high seas in the eighteenth century, and about explorers in the nineteenth century. Work-hunting seemed just like that to Sam. Bold, fearless and wild. Work-hunters were the swashbuckling adventurers of the twenty-first century, that's what Sam reckoned. And his Dad was one of them. His Dad was a hero.

Sometimes, Dad's band were away for many weeks, sometimes for only a day or two. Sam would be the first at the front door on their return.

There would be hugs and laughing, lots of talk amongst the adults and, if things had gone well on the hunt, presents for the youngsters. After the initial flurry of noise and voices, the band would settle down for a few days rest before going back to work.

Sam would always be the first to ask questions. "What did you all do this time, Dad?" "Where did you go?" "Did you see any interesting places?"

The last time the band came home, they brought all sorts of new equipment for the house with them: an upgraded Netlink, a second freeze-storage chamber to place underground in the garden for keeping food fresh, and an assortment of odds and ends. All these things were bonuses they'd earnt on their latest job. They'd been working for a month on a new office building in Birmingham, Dad installing Net systems, the others organizing the renting of desks or the moving of workers into the building from another part of the city. Dad's band were Certified 2★V, which is what was printed on the ID badges they had to wear, and which meant that they did jobs which were technical or which supervised others.

Sam's family couldn't afford to pay for him to go to a real school, or consult anything but the Web Home Medical Databank when he was ill, but even so, Sam counted himself lucky. They were better off than a lot of people.

He'd read an article on the Netlink recently about kids his age, like him, who'd never been to a real school because of the cost, or been to real places because of the security restrictions. It had said that kids like him grew up with a twisted and unrealistic view of the world, and of how they fitted into it. Sam thought that was utter rubbish.

He sat on the step of the conservatory, feeling the mid-day summer heat glow against him. On roaring hot days like this he couldn't even remember the slicing cold of the long ice-bound winters. But winter would come around again, as it always did, and all too soon.

That last time Dad came home, he'd trudged through the house, shedding his backpack and his heavy shoes, greeting everyone with a kiss or a pick-you-off-the-floor bearhug. Sam had danced around him as he went, and when it was his turn for a hello, he clung tightly around Dad's neck and told him he was so pleased to have him back again.

"I'm glad too," said Dad. The edges of his eyes folded up as he smiled, just like Sam's did.

"Tell me all about it," said Sam. "What did you all do this time Dad?"

"Ooh, steady on," said Dad. "Later on, okay? Let me sit down for a minute."

Dad always seemed to say that on his return from

work. Always.

Dad had an oily smell about him. He and the band had driven home with a gang of workers from a meat factory. Mum didn't stop complaining about the pong for two days.

For much of the rest of that day, right up until Sam's bedtime, Dad was slumped in his favourite chair, quietly dozing. Sam wanted to wake him up and ask him things, but Mum said "Sam, shhh! No, your father's been at work, and he's very tired. There'll be plenty of time to ask him things later."

Sam gradually pieced together the information on Dad's office job in Birmingham through things Dad mentioned to Mum and the others that day.

"Dad, can I go to see the office you worked on?"

"Hmm?" said Dad, looking up from his supper. "No, I'm sorry, Sam, you wouldn't be allowed in."

"Or could we visit the computers in Japan you sorted out a while ago?"

"What? No, we can't. Why would you want to?"

Sam wanted to because… well, because the pictures in his head of his Dad at work couldn't be as exciting as the real thing, could they? Surely, the real thing was even more thrillingly adventurous?

Sam could see how tired Dad was after a long job away from home. So Dad must surely have been the hardest working work-hunter there.

Sam could see the scuffs on Dad's shoes and coat. So Dad must have got into some pretty daring and dangerous situations.

Sam could hear the phone calls Dad made to other work-hunters, and to people he'd worked for in the past. So Dad must be highly skilled. Someone in demand. Someone others called on in a crisis. A troubleshooter. The one they called on when all else had failed.

Sam talked about his deductions to cousin Sophie the next morning. She smirked, like older girls her age always seemed to, and shook her head. "You keep dreamin', kiddo," she said. "Your dad's tired because they work him like a dog. His shoes are scuffed 'cos they're old. And he's always on his phone because… that's what work-hunters do. They hunt for work."

Sam thought Sophie was just being grouchy, as usual. He much preferred his own explanations for things. His own explanations fitted the facts better. Or so he reckoned, anyway. In all the detective stories he read, those were the conclusions that the hero would have come to, so there.

"Dad, can I try on your coat?"

"But it wouldn't fit you, Sam."

"I know."

"I'm sorry, I need it, I've got to go out in a minute."

"Can't I wear it until you come back?"

"Sam, without the cooler units in my coat I'll roast out there!" Dad looked down at him. He looked up at Dad. Dad kind of wriggled and sighed. "Look, Sam, I'm sorry, I know you want to hear all about what I've been doing, but I've got to go and see someone about my next job. I can't not go. We'll talk about it later, yeah? When I get back. I promise."

Sam paused for a moment or two. "Okay," he said with a flat smile.

He knew there was no point arguing. If he argued, Dad would get as grumpy as Sophie, and Sam would probably not get a chance to talk to him until it was time for him to go again!

Dad was gone for a couple of hours. In that time, Sam and his mum rooted all the insects out of the garden with a beam-splitter that Dad had brought home as part of his bonus.

"Dad probably won't have to go off to work again for a week or two," said Mum. "There'll be plenty of time to do things together before that. Plenty of time later."

"I s'pose so," grumbled Sam.

"Sam," said Mum, "your dad loves you very much, and I love you very much, you know that. But… we're all busy. Everyone's busy at something, we have to be, to keep the house and all of us going, don't we? You know that too. It's just that… Dad's busy… away from home. That's all. Please try to understand. He's not trying to be awkward."

"He's just busy," said Sam quietly.

"Exactly," said Mum. She hugged him, and gave him a kiss on his forehead. "You're a big grown-up boy, and I'm proud of you," she whispered, her lips close to his hair.

Sam thought that if he was grown-up enough to understand about grown-ups' busy lives, then surely he was grown-up enough to be given the same time as they gave each other. But he said nothing.

Dad was in a bad mood when he got back. Whoever he'd gone to see about a job hadn't given him the answers he'd expected. You didn't need to be a detective to work that one out.

Even so, a promise was a promise. "Dad?"

"What is it?"

"You said you'd tell me about your adventures when you got back."

Dad let out a long, slow breath. "Yes. Yes I did," he said. "And I will. Just let me calm down a bit. I'm having a pig of a day, okay? Ask me again later."

Sam turned and walked away. He went back into the kitchen where Mum and Auntie Jo were doing the tea.

Sam didn't ask again later. Deliberately, to see if Dad would remember. He didn't, or at least he didn't appear to.

It wasn't that he was being awkward. He was just busy.

Then, shortly before bedtime, Sam couldn't bear the suspense any longer. He found Dad at the computer in the living room.

"Dad?"

"Hmm?"

"You said later."

Dad didn't look away from the screen. "Later what?"

"You'd tell me about everything you'd been doing at work?"

Dad paused for a moment. Slowly, he bounced a fist against his head a couple of times, then swung around in his chair. "Yes, I know. Why didn't you remind me? It's far too late now."

"I could stay up late."

"No, you couldn't. You need your sleep. We'll talk in the morning, yeah?"

Sam turned on his heels and went upstairs to bed without another word. While he was reading, by the light of his bedside lamp, he heard Mum and Dad talking in the hallway downstairs. He couldn't quite make out what they were saying, so he slid off his bed and opened the door of his room a crack. He put his ear to the gap.

"Are you sure?" said Mum.

"You saw the email! If we're not getting that other job I have to take this one. If I'm not there tomorrow, we'll lose the whole deal. Susanna and the others can follow me in a day or two, but I'll have to leave first thing in the morning. I'm sorry."

"Oh well," sighed Mum. "The money will see us through the winter."

Sam felt a knot of anger tighten through his insides. So Dad was off again, was he? For a split second, Sam thought about rushing down the stairs and asking if he could go with Dad this time, just this one time, he wouldn't make a fuss, or get in the way, could he, could he, just this once, pleeeeeease?

For a split second. He knew that trying anything like that was pointless.

He sat on his bed for a few minutes, thinking. Nothing occurred to him until he heard the electronic hum of the Family Archive android coming up the stairs. That would be Grandma, and Grandad George, and all the other contents of the Archive wanting to get a little shut-eye.

They had retired. They were dead. They had all the time in the world, thought Sam.

And time was the one thing Dad never seemed to find.

He sat very still for a few minutes more, thinking through the idea that had just popped into his head.

The beam-splitter that he and Mum had been using in the garden was propped against his bedside cabinet. He'd hung onto it, in case the nest of waspivores from next door's roof started getting peckish for human plasma in the night.

It was small and light. The size of an unimpressive carrot.

At last, making up his mind, he picked up the beam-splitter and crept out of his room. There was a light on in the living room, but not in the kitchen. He could tiptoe down the stairs and across the hall without too much risk of being spotted.

His heart was thumping as he stepped... slowly, slowly... down into the hall. Did he have a cover story if someone heard him creeping about? No, he didn't. But he was concentrating too hard on the job in hand to worry about that now.

The tiled hall floor was cool against his feet. Dad's coat was on the pegs by the door, in its usual spot. Sam nestled up against it, as if he could hide behind it if Mum were to suddenly emerge from the living room. As if she wouldn't see his legs sticking out!

Dad's dark, heavy coat still smelt slightly of the wild outdoors. Cities, windy landscapes, crowds.

Sam bent and found a small rip in the coat's lining, at the back, right at the bottom edge. Without hesitating, he slipped the beam-splitter into the rip and it dropped down into the lining, out of sight.

He scampered back to bed, zipping with excitement. Quick, quick, before somebody saw!

The beam-splitter would get Dad home early. Sam had done a lot of reading about the cities, and he'd done a teleschool project on homeland security not long ago. The beam-splitter would be detected in the coat lining at one checkpoint or another. The police would start by asking questions: Why was it there? What was Dad going to do with it? Why had he hidden it?

Then what? What would a daring adventurer like Dad do? The police would be very cross with him. There might even be a valiant escape!

Of course, the point was that Dad would get turned away from wherever he was going. He would have to come home early. He would have more time.

Dad would be pleased, in the end, thought Sam. Daring adventurers deserved time off too, didn't they? Dad was always so tired when he got home, so pushed for time. And anyway, what was the point of having daring adventures for years if you didn't stop at some point and tell everyone all about them?

He tucked himself up in bed, and slept soundly. By the time he woke up, Dad had gone to work.

All that was a couple of days ago now. Sam sat on the step of the conservatory, in the heat of the early afternoon, wondering what stories Dad would have to tell when he got back.

Sooner than expected. Hee hee. Couldn't be long now, surely?

Sam went into the house, blinking as his eyes adjusted to the shade. The android-as-Grandma was sitting at the kitchen table, flicking through a magazine on the Netlink.

"You look jolly pleased with yourself, young Sam," said the android-as-Grandma with a smile.

"I am, Grandma," said Sam. "I am."

Mum answered the phone. Her voice started calm, but got gradually more and more hysterical.

They'll be turning him around and sending him home. Hee hee. Sam was sure of that. No need to wait for later. Time for stories of adventure.

Mum yelled to Auntie Jo to link up the Family Archive android to Police Sequencer 2. There was panic about a security breach, and police action, and an execution in two minutes' time.

And an…? Sam felt a sudden gaping sensation inside.

The android-as-Grandma shuffled uneasily. "Oh dear, Sam, what could have happened? Is someone going to join us in this archive unexpectedly?"

"Mum!" cried Sam. "Aren't they just sending him home? What about his valiant escape?"

Mum could barely speak above her fear. "Don't be

STUPID, Sam! How do you think the world works, you silly little... JO! Link up the android! NOW!"

Auntie Jo yanked at the android's arm, switching it into Receive mode, dragging it to the nearest Netlink port.

Dad is an adventurer. They don't do that to heroic adventurers. They just don't.

Dad's coming home. He must be coming home. Mustn't he? The screaming, empty hole in Sam's insides got wider, and deeper, and darker.

Yes. Yes. There'll be plenty of time to talk about it later.

Later.

# Whooosh!

## DANIEL WEITZMAN

**W**eek 1.

"What do you think of your mother's re-marriage?" asked Dad, resisting the temptation to tuck me into bed. His bed. Wednesday night is his night, which means I get his bed. In his house. On his side of town. He claims not to mind sleeping on the couch, and I have a funny feeling he actually is okay with it – having slept on the couch just about every night when he and Mom were still together. Oh, they'd both pretend Dad was still sleeping in the bedroom, with Mom – but I could tell it wasn't true… that big dent in the couch said it all; as did the bottle of seltzer he almost always left on the coffee table.

"I don't know, Dad… what do you think?" I bounced the question back at the Dad-Man, totally not wanting to level with him. If he knew what I really think, he'd worry, and I don't want that. First of all, there's nothing he can do about it; it's not like he's a master of personality transplants; he can't wish an even worse personality onto Tim (my mom's fiancé) to help Mom see what a huge mistake she's making. Second of all, if I tell him, it's like the last straw, the thing that says to me that this whole thing is real. That Mom is marrying that big dufus and ditching Dad for good.

"Honestly?" Dad looked at me with fish-eyes: a cold, hard stare that hides the tears because it's under water. Maybe he wasn't on the verge of crying, but I wanted to think he was. As always, I was getting mad for Dad. If only he'd screamed back at Mom, maybe they could've made it. Seems to me she likes a good fight; I have a better shot at getting my way with her when I give her a hard time than when I roll over. Except, of course, in the current matter.

"No Dad, lie to me." Dad smiled – a real deal smile. Not the kind of smile that shows up when he thinks he should smile, the kind that just happens.

"Honestly, I think it sucks." His smile was gone before I'd even begun to dig on it, little crinkly creases straightening it out before it had a chance to breathe.

Leave it to Dad to wait until something's in your face before he deals with it. Mom and Tim's wedding was just six weeks away, and while I kept thinking something would get in the way – something like my dad – it suddenly became clear to me, clear as the high-def TV Timmy talked my mother into buying. Like okay, it's cool and all, but here she's always ragging on Dad for not giving her enough money for me, and then she goes out and scores a high-def? Definitely not cool.

Anyway, it was clear as clear could be.

Dad wasn't going to do anything about Mom and Timmy.

"She actually invited me to the wedding," said Dad, swallowing the last few words.

"You're not going, are you?" My turn to pull a fish. "Not that I don't want you, but—"

"I wouldn't come within a hundred miles," exclaimed Dad, eyes now flashing, maybe even angry.

Did you ever notice how loud silence can be? Dad's room suddenly screamed the big empties. I couldn't help but notice – like I had every week for three years – that Dad still had a picture of Mom by the bed. The two of them, at a happier time: sunset, overlooking some mountain path. Mom with flowers in her hair, dad with no white hairs in his. Real deal smiles all around. I guess I don't have to tell you that Mom has no such picture by her bed, and it isn't because of Timmy. The pictures were long gone before The Timster showed up, him and his bad breath and his super baggy pants. I swear, if I see his butt-crack one more time, I'm going to shove a lamp in it.

Maybe not.

Point is, Mom has so checked out on Dad that she doesn't even like talking to him any more. Inviting him to the wedding? Betcha that was Timmy's bright idea. Had to be, no question. Mom scarcely knows Dad exists any more.

That doesn't work for me.

So I've got six weeks to come up with something, six weeks to get them back together.

Any ideas?

👨👨👨👨👨

*Week 2.*

"Dad, have you thought about getting your hair cut?" I knew what he'd say, but I had to put it out there anyway. Mom had become waaaaay tired of Dad's left-over rock 'n' roller image; something about wanting him to look more business-y. I can't stand how she considers him such a failure; what has Timmy ever done to rate? Far as I can tell – not much – except re-heat pizza. Another thing: Dad loves his hair; even though long white strands are a little bit on the warlock side, I've got to say – I'm a fan too. Still, if it gets Mom to take another look at Dad, maybe a haircut isn't such a bad idea.

"Edward, I know what you're doing." Check that – it's a *terrible* idea.

"What? What am I doing?" Playing dumb was my only possible defense; I've got to say, it came to me a little bit too easily. So, okay, I'm no genius; I've still got a job to do. I mean, here we are – five weeks away

150

from The Big Disaster, and I'm getting nowhere. Fast. Hence, the haircut idea.

"You're trying to make me more attractive to your mother."

"Dad, if she doesn't like you the way you are, then what do you need her for?" Hey – who's a better ally than me?

"That's kind of what I thought," said Dad, manning his bedside perch. I dug further into his bed.

"This isn't easy for you, is it?" Dad – love you – but sometimes, you're no genius, either.

"I love my Wednesday nights, Dad."

"You know what I mean, Edward – is it Timothy?"

"No." Much as I rag on him (behind his back), it really isn't Timmy – "Timothy," as Dad calls him. I can't explain it. It's this feeling that like my dad is a balloon, that the wind will – *whooosh!* – just take him away from me. I'll be watching as he gets smaller and smaller, disappearing into a cloud of twice-a-week get togethers and alternating summer vacations.

Okay, so I'm a little bit on the dramatic side. You try being a divorced kid. It does stuff to you. Even though Dad makes a point of picking me up at school at least twice a week, of coming to all my soccer games, of talking to me on the phone every day we're not together, it's still not the same.

Makes me miss those wild arguments with Mom.

Well, not quite.

I remember walking into Dad's apartment when this was all new; dad says to me:

"Make yourself at home." Then he checks himself. "You *are* home, Edward," he follows with. Cute, huh? Can you blame me for trying to hang onto that balloon?

"So, what is it?" said Dad.

"You don't understand, Dad."

"Not unless you tell me." Like I said, the man's no genius.

"I just wish—"

"Uh, oh – this is going to be good."

"If you want to skip it…" My toes dug into his freshly-changed sheets. Dad's place may be home, but sometimes it feels like a hotel. Dude even hits me up with chocolate before I go to bed, though he doesn't leave it on his pillow. And he doesn't exactly encourage pillow fights.

"No, I don't want to skip it." The man on the edge of the bed looked positively menacing. Yeah, right. Dad couldn't hurt a fly, wouldn't.

"Okay," I said, toes digging in even deeper, "but this might hurt a little bit."

"If you don't think I can handle it by now…" Once again, Dad swallowed the end of his sentence. I wondered if I should eat my words, eat them before spitting them out.

"Dad, I think you should go back to being a dentist."

Silence again. The big empties.

"I wonder if you understand, Edward." Ouch. That one hurt. Me.

"I know you hated it, Dad—"

"Do you?"

"It's just that, well, it's just that…" Like father, like son. I couldn't finish my thought, didn't dare.

"If you think your mother will take me back because I've got a regular nine-to-five…"

"I'm sorry, Dad." And I was. Really sorry. Sorry to have opened my big mouth, sorry to be in this stupid situation. "I shouldn't have said anything. I'm sure the writing thing will work out." After you're dead. After Mom and Timmy have made it official. After my life turns to complete and total crapola.

"I don't know that it will, son." I know something's up when he calls me "son". Upset, angry – something's always up with "son". "I might just fall on my big, fat ugly face," says Dad, not batting an eyelash.

"You're not afraid?"

"I'm afraid not to try." Okay, that sounds good and all – a real Dad-ism ("Mom-ism," if it comes from her mouth) – but what does it mean?

"It *has* been a while, Dad." Jeez, guy, why don't

you just sock Dad right in the face?

"You're right, Edward," said Dad, unleashing a sigh. "And it could be a while longer. Meanwhile, I don't think you've missed too many meals." Double-ouch – the ol' You're Really a Child of Privilege Rap. Ask me how privileged I feel!

"Whatever makes you happy, Dad…"

"Believe it or not, Ed – making you happy is what makes me happy."

"Know what, Dad?"

"What?"

"I'm kind of tired."

"Yeah," said Dad, rolling off the bed, "me too." He leaned over to tuck me in, caught himself. "Ooops. Sorry."

"It's alright, Dad." And it was. So it's a little retarded for a twelve-year-old. I felt like I needed it. Dad tucked me in, grinned the goofy grin of someone who was putting one over on me.

Haircut, my butt. Why would I want to make Dad over, anyway?

♦♦♦♦♦

*Week 3.*

Another week. No progress to report. How do you bring together two people who really don't want to be together? Is it incredibly selfish of me to be pushing for this? Dad seems to be getting on, and

Mom – well, Mom has her Timster. I can knock him all I want – and I do – but the Momster is smiling more than she was when she was with Dad.

Still, the thought of doing the Divorced Shuffle forever and a day is enough to make my mouth go dry, give me cotton-brain.

"You feeling okay?"

Dad gives me the customary bedtime stare, feels my forehead with his palm. "No temperature," he says, hand plopping into his lap. That one always gets me. Technically, I *do* have a temperature, should be around ninety nine big degrees.

I merely shrug, my latest strategy coming into play.

"You want something to drink?"

Another shrug.

"One last chocolate before lights out?" Man, you'd think the guy had never been a dentist. Or maybe this is just his revenge for all the years of foul-breathed fillings and drillings.

Another shrug.

"Oh, I get it," says dad. At least somebody does. "You want to be inducted into the Fart-Face Hall of Fame?" Dad can't think I'm going to fall for that one; a strategy is a strategy. I shrug again.

"The Silent Treatment, Edward? How *old* is that?"

Shrug.

I can see the muscles in Dad's arm – the few that

he has, not exactly being a pumping iron type –
relax. The creases in his brow go flat. He taps his
fingers, looks away. Shrugs. Shrugs again.

I shrug back at him.

Great, this week's breakthrough: a Shrug-off.

Dad takes it one step further, sprawls across his bed,
opposite me: his feet where my head is, my feet where
– well, approaching, anyway – where his head is.

No way am I going to tell him what I've been
through this past week: shopping for the wedding,
dragged to some horrible store just so I can "look
nice" for Mom's Big Day. I don't mind the tie and
jacket that much; maybe there's a touch of the Spifster
in me, but I sure hate the shoes. Stiff, black; they feel
like they're ten thousand pounds each, like they're
sucking my whole body in. I don't understand the
whole deal behind dress-up – though on the plus
side, losing the super baggy pants should stop Timmy's
butt showing for at least a couple hours.

"Why did the chicken cross the road?"

I shrug.

"The rhino?"

Shrug.

"The sabretoothed tiger?" Yeah, Dad – that'll work;
kids always respond to dino-like creatures. With a shrug.

I wonder what Dad will do on the day of The Big
Disaster. Write? Tube-out? Laundry? Shrug? Will he

think about Mom and what's to come? Or will he flash back to when he was still with her, we were all still together? Knowing Dad, he'll think forwards and backwards – then not at all. Shut down. Shut in. System failure. Maybe he'll storm the gates, protest? "Does anybody here know of any reason why these two should not be joined in holy matrimony?" When the priest asks, maybe Dad'll pop out of an aisle seat, object to Tim's chromosomal structure, or his collection of Alice Cooper records. Even a diehard rock guy like my dad knows that A Cooper is like nowhere, that things have come a long way since the days of mascara music.

"Why did *I* cross the road?" That one is at least tempting. To avoid Mom? To get back with Mom? To watch one of my soccer games? Translation: shrug.

"Because I couldn't cross my t's…" Now, *that* is hurt. Low blow, Dad. I manage not to groan, not easy.

"Not even a groan?" Dad's eyes narrow, disappointed. Doesn't he realize what's at stake here? Doesn't he see, see that he's been traded in for this year's model?

I can't wait for Mom and Timmy to start arguing. Door-slamming. Throwing things at each other. At least they're too old to have more kids.

I think.

I hope.

I pray.

That would be like the totally last straw. Timmy Jr. Or Tammy. Or the Timmy and Tammy twins. Dad and I would have even more in common: Mom wouldn't know either of us existed.

I've really got to get working on this.

"Not even a little whimper?" says Dad. "That was a *terrible* joke."

I shrug.

"That's it, I've had it!" Dad says, jumping up, blowing out of my room. His room. Our room. "I know this really good child psychologist…"

"No, Dad – no shrinks!" I jump up.

"He speaks!" Dad turns, eyeballs me. "I knew that one would work."

"You don't seem to realize what we're up against here, Dad." I eyeball him right back, not happy eyeballs.

"So, you don't mind seeing a shrink?"

"I do mind. I live with a shrink six days a week – in case you don't remember."

Dad shrugs, this one innocent. "I remember." He laughs.

I laugh. Why not? The crapola's just going to keep coming.

And I always have next week.

†††††

*Week 4.*

"That was not acceptable," says Dad, glaring at me.

Guess I deserved it.

Not half an hour earlier, Dad had plucked me from the rafters of the local electronics store, where I was sort of hiding out.

Well, not sort of. Definitely.

I saw him storm into the place, looking around like a crazy man. Didn't know if I should come clean or morph into one of the nearby plasma screens.

I did neither. No action. Inaction. Bump on a log. Too scared to come forwards, too scared to look for a better hiding spot.

If I learned anything this afternoon, it's that running away from home (*either* home) may require some actual running.

Anyway, Dad spots me, goes into full-tilt sprint. About ten feet away from me, he slows down, waaaaay down, and like saunters up to me.

"See anything you like?" he says, real wise-ass. "Maybe a new TV?" I freak, thinking that maybe he knows about the high-def at Mom's. But outwardly, nothing. I just kind of look around, give him some wise-ass back. "I was looking for the frozen foods section," I say.

"Pistachio?" Dad plays along with me. "Or should I just *cream* you?" For the moment. He makes a fist, airboxes my ears, a little too close for comfort.

What does he know about comfort, anyway – as

in, *my* comfort... If he really cared about me, wouldn't he just work it out with Mom?

Or is that just a kid-ism?

Whatever. I *am* a kid, am entitled to a few stupid sayings, thinkings – even if I don't say, think them out loud.

"You want a little something?" says Dad, indicating the rows full of tekkie toys. "Maybe a new video game?"

Guess I should run away more often.

"I can?"

"You can." Dad shakes his head. "Not that you deserve it, but…"

I don't wait for him to change his mind, jump on the nearest game.

"Break-Out?" Dad looks it over, sees the picture of some maximum security monsters burrowing out from underground. "Couldn't we go with something… something more…?" He looks at me, sees me in all my bright-eyed splendour. "Break-Out it is," he sighs, nudging me towards the checkout line.

"Can we get some pistachio too?"

"Don't push your luck," says Dad, giving me a real dad look. I stand in line alongside Dad, pretty much happy as can be, my whole dilemma momentarily forgotten.

As always, happiness doesn't hang around for me –

though it looks like it could – and for Dad.
For there, in line, scooching in right behind us,
is this really cute girl.

Check that: *woman.*

Not that I'm an expert on women – don't want
to be – but this one, this one is A-okay: long dark
hair, tall, the kind of face that looks like it knows
how to smile, maybe because it *is* smiling.

At me.

"What's your name?" says the smile.

"Edward," I yelp, yelp like a stupid little puppy dog.

"I'm thinking you're about fourteen?" Man, she's
getting cuter by the second.

"Twelve, actually," I say, more like screech.
Between you, me and everybody in the store, I've
never had a girlfriend. Girls are just so, so… girl-y.

"My cousin's turning twelve," she dips into her
shopping cart, pulls out a CD-ROM. "Think he'd
like this?"

My turn to be the balloon, all the air
*WHOOOSHING* out of me. Only I stay firmly on
the ground. All of a sudden, I have a great idea.
World-class. And it's not to suggest a different CD.

"Daaaad, what do you think?" I turn to The Man,
give him his nudge back.

"How would I know?" The Man is clueless.

"Your son is very cute." Great – she's running

with it – but does she have to call me "cute"?

"You want our place in line?" I'm like the Knight In White Shining Armour.

Anything to get Dad thinking about women again. Maybe Mom will get super-jealous, drop Tim like a hot potato. Okay, it's a stretch, but once again, I plead The Kid, a kid with a real situation on his hands.

"No, I'm good." I swear, she's smiling at Dad. More like beaming. C'mon, Big Guy – you can do it: ask her her name, or suggest some other CD-ROM – make it up if you have to.

Dad smiles, super-polite, says nothing. Do I have to do all the work around here?

"We're just doing a little shopping," I say, back to the shrug. "Food's next, maybe some ice cream." Who's smoother than me? "Mom used to do the shopping, but now my mom and dad are divorced."

What follows is maybe the loudest silence in the history of silence.

"You have to excuse my son," says Dad, totally not excusing me. "He has some very definite opinions about my social life."

"Like I said," says the woman, bouncing her hair very girly-ish. "He's very cute." She shrugs. "And you're not bad, either." Is it my imagination, or does she wink at Dad?

"I'm flattered," says Dad. "But I'm kind of in a

holding pattern right now."

Why do I even try?

†††††

*Week 5.*

We're really cutting it close here. A week and a half until The Big Disaster.

You'd never know it from checking out my Dad.

"Nathan hopped from wisp to wisp, trying to find a toehold…" Dad's idea of a bedtime story hadn't changed in like forever. Problem with writer-types, they think everything that comes out of their mouths is so incredibly genius. While Dad's stories aren't like the worst thing in the world, they aren't necessarily the best either.

"The Cloud People" was one of my least faves; not that I've ever told Dad, but if there's one thing that's sure to put me to sleep, it's *this* dad tale.

"If you've ever tried climbing a cloud, you know how few and far between toeholds are," said Dad. Where's your toehold, Dad? What are you going to do once you really realize that Mom is gone? Once *I* realize it? Does the concept of *too* late mean anything to you? "The Cloud People" wasn't going to put me to sleep **this** night. I couldn't afford to sleep.

"Dad?"

He gave me a look, a look that said something like, "How dare you interrupt Mr Shakespeare".

"Yes?" Oh, joy. Dagger Eyes.

"I was wondering…"

"Yes?" Really sharp Dagger Eyes.

"I was wondering if maybe I could tell a story?"

"Now?" Amazingly, the Dagger Eyes weren't so sharp any more.

"Yeah, now."

"As long as it's not better than my story…"

"We won't know until we hear it…"

"I'm all ears…" Dad kicked back, made a gesture like "bring it on".

I brought it on.

"Once upon a time—"

"Oh, that's really original." I gave Dad my version of Dagger Eyes, pushed on.

"Once upon a time, there was this father and this son."

"Oh, no…"

"Do you think you could not interrupt for like five minutes?"

"Sorry."

"Anyway, this father and this son were really tight. This father knew all this son's likes and dislikes—"

"Likes," dad chimed in, "chocolate, video games, tropical fish." Suddenly, we were telling this story together. I couldn't help but nod. "Dislikes: carrots, homework, shoelace-tieing." Another nod. My turn.

"And this son knew all this father's likes and dislikes." The story-telling dance was a little cutesy, but between you, me – and you and me – I was kind of digging on it. "Likes," – I gave dad the once over, just sort of let it fly – "coffee, The Classics, going barefoot." Say hello to dad's goofy grin. "Dislikes: Plaque, 'Best Of' Albums, backtalk." Dad's turn to nod. Did we know each other, or what?

"Anyway, they were really tight, there was a really good thing between this father and this son," I said, scrambling to change the course of history – history that hadn't happened – yet. "Only this father and this son were missing a little something."

Dad groaned. "I wonder what that could be," he said. "I can't imagine you mean a trampoline in the living room."

"No," I managed something like a smile, maybe 50% real deal. "Though that wouldn't suck."

"Edward." Oops. Another of Dad's dislikes? Swear words – when *I* swear them. "How's it going with the wedding, anyway?" End of that story. I had a few more swear words in mind, but held off. Barely.

"Okay, I guess."

"Your mother called last night."

Whoa. Pinch me, people. Could this be a real breakthrough? Was Mom reaching out to Dad? Was there a shot she was coming to her senses? "She wanted to know if I was coming." No shot.

"You're not, right?"

"Right."

"Wouldn't come within a thousand miles, right, Dad?"

"I think it was, 'a hundred'."

"Whatever."

On the bedside table, I caught the picture of my mom and dad and the mountain path. Why couldn't things still be like that?

Why?

Why?

Why?

One thing was for sure. Dad could stay his hundred miles away from the wedding. I would go for a thousand.

*♀♂♀♂♀*

*Week 6.*

"World-class, huh?" Dad spooned up the last of his pistachio scream, the spoon scraping against the side of the bowl with an annoying "TRRRR".

Maybe I was a little sensitive; can you blame me? Here I am, a few days away from the worst possible thing that could happen to me – not counting Mom and Dad's divorce – and the Dad-Man's eating ice cream like it's just another day. Lying in bed next to me, in fact – staring up at the ceiling. I wonder what he sees there: the future? A cockroach? More cockroaches in his future?

"It's okay," I said, my spoon quietly smooshing through scream. Normally, I would've been onto seconds by now, but for reasons you can probably guess, I wasn't that hungry. Even the cookie crumble on top of my scoop wasn't revving up my appetite.

Six weeks earlier, I had set out on a mission.

Six weeks later, I had failed miserably.

Dad and Mom would not be getting back together – no way, no how. I couldn't put Humpty Dumpty together again. Crapola ruled. Pathetic: that I was doomed to have a stepfather with the intelligence of a fruit roll-up. That I would be doing the Divorced Shuffle forever and a day. That I actually thought I could pull it off, be like the magic healing dude that brings people together.

Yeah, right.

Perched on my chest, a little green swimming pool invited me in for a dip, but my spoon wasn't going anywhere.

And neither was my brain.

My butt, on the other hand, was doomed to show up at St Bartholomew's that coming Sunday. Totally dressed up. The ten thousand pound shoes. The hair combed. The ears cleaned. Tie and jacket.

I put my ice cream down, rolled over on my

side. Away from Dad. Why couldn't he fight this thing? Did he not care what I wanted? Was he like so totally oblivious?

I felt him get up, heard his feet hit the floor.

"Goodnight," I said, just wanting to get the whole thing over with. All of a sudden, I was like so totally tired. Eyelids felt heavier than my fancy shoes.

"Before you knock off, there's something I should probably show you," said Dad. I heard the creak of the closet door. What was Dad going to drag out, was he up to his usual too-little, too-late strategy? *You* bring it on, Dad, break out the crazy corpse that's been hanging around in there since you moved in. Was it there when you got here, or did you bury it?

"Here, check it out." I was tempted to fake sleep, but opted out. How often did Dad reach out to me like that? Okay, so granted – he's no stranger to sharing stuff with me, but still, there was something about his voice, something that said "son".

I rolled back the other way to see what was up...

Funny how you don't realize how great somebody is when they're kind of around, part of your life. My Dad. Maybe a hundred miles from Mom, but right in my face.

"You should probably learn how to do this." Dad twirled the ends of a tie that was looped around his neck, a blue tie, blue with red and yellow stripes.

"That?" I was more than a little surprised, and not just because my dad's like the last person to wear a tie.

"For this weekend, Edward." Right you are, Dad. That would be the weekend in question.

"I know which weekend it is, Dad." He plopped the tie around my neck, started fiddling.

"I'll cut you some slack with the shoelaces, Ed – but the tie, the tie has to be tied."

Even though I really didn't want to, I sat up. Something about the voice kept talking to me… this father, this son, this has got to be heard.

"Then you flop this end over this end." Dad did some more fiddling, a crossover, a pull-through… presto chango, I was The Spifster, weekend-ready, a vision of ridiculousness in my pjs and a tie.

"Beautiful." Dad admired his handiwork.

Of course, I would never remember how to pull off the tie thing by Sunday, but that was beside the point. The point was that I was all of a sudden okay with the marriage thing. Not like happy overjoyed okay. But okay.

If dad could learn how to deal, I realized I could too.

Timmy would become my mother's husband. But he wasn't becoming my Dad.

I already had one.

And I wasn't letting go.

# Street Corner Dad

## ALAN GIBBONS

*With thanks to Maisie Long for the loan of bits of her life*

It never occurred to me that we would ever be apart. Even when the bombs started falling on Liverpool I didn't think they would make any difference to my family. I was born in 1930, I was nine when the War started, living in Bond Street, just off Scotland Road. There were five of us in a three bedroomed kitchen house. We were lucky, luckier than the two bedroomed ones across the tenement staircase. We had a hot water tap and a bath. All they had was the cold water tap.

Nan ran the house with a rod of iron. Kathleen, her name was and everybody was in fear of her. She had a face like a hawk and a liking for Guinness. Mam and Dad had the second room though Dad was often away on his ship. He was a seaman, part of the battle of the Atlantic, trying to break the Nazi blockade and keep Britain going through the darkest part of the War. Nan never liked him. She didn't think he was good enough for her daughter. Me and Molly made do with the box room. Molly was five. She was always whining and her nose ran non-stop.

We were happy though most people today would wonder what we had to be happy about. Most nights the air raid siren would wail through the mist and we would take ourselves off to the shelter in The Swings. This was open ground with maypoles, a bandstand and two kinds of shelter: one underground and one visible above ground and made of brick. One time a land mine was found unexploded in The Swings. The houses had to be cleared for three days and we all slept in St Martin's Hall.

The funny thing is we kids took it in our stride. We ran wild too. When lots of the other kids were evacuated to North Wales, Nan said we weren't going.

"If it happens, it happens," she said. "At least we'll all go together."

That was that. Anything Nan said was gospel. Mam never once stood up to her in her life. Dad loved Mam so he did what she wanted. That's how we, along with a few other kids in the neighbourhood, ended up sticking it out at home. For months there wasn't even any school. There just weren't enough kids to make it worthwhile. When school did start again it was in somebody's front room. You went for a morning but you didn't learn much. Not that me or Molly cared. We just wanted to go about our bother. Like I said, we were happy.

Then it happened.

The evening started with Nan laying down the law.

"You're not going down that dance hall tonight," she said.

"Oh, come on Kathleen," Dad said. "We just want to enjoy ourselves. I'm away to sea tomorrow."

"You never know what might happen," Nan said, always ready to have a go at him.

"That's a bit rich, isn't it?" Dad said. "You're the one who didn't want the kids evacuated."

Nan scowled and said they were fools to go. Dad just grinned and swept Mam out the door. I could hear their laughter fading into the night. That's the last time I saw them together. The next day grey-faced men filled the parlour and Nan sat in her chair, her hawk's face white and her black eyes on Dad. He just sat in the corner, his shoulders hunched. It was as though somebody had ripped the life out of him. He sat like a puppet with its strings cut. It was a while before I understood. They'd been in St Bridget's church hall when a bomb hit. Some people were killed there, but not Mam. She cheated death the first time. She was taken to Mill Road hospital to be treated for a minor head wound. It was a million-to-one chance that the hospital would be hit in the same raid, but in war million-to-one chances happen. She died in the hospital where they're supposed to make people better.

Days later, even while the pain was still fresh, I was woken by angry voices. One was Dad's. The other belonged to Nan. As I crept to the door, there was a splinter lodged in my heart. I already knew what this was about but I hoped against hope I was wrong.

"Get out!" Nan was screaming. "Go away to sea and don't ever come sniffing round this door again."

I wanted to cry out, tell her he was my dad and she had no right to talk to him that way. But the words stuck in my throat. I watched them, black figures silhouetted against the morning sunlight that was shining through the open door.

"You can't keep me away," Dad said quietly. "Jimmy and Molly are mine. I've a right to see them."

That's when Nan said words I'll never forget.

"You killed my daughter," she said. "I'll raise her kids. You…"

She stabbed a bony finger at the street.

"You'll get on your ship and I hope you go down with it. Yes, I hope the U-boats take you to the bottom of the sea."

But Dad wasn't done yet. Seeing me looking round the door, he shoved past Nan and strode towards me. His jacket smelled of salt and tobacco.

He stroked Molly's hair while she was still sleeping, then he spoke to me.

"I'm sorry you had to hear that, Jimmy," he said. "I've got to go away, but I'll be back for you, both of you."

Then he glanced at Nan to make sure she wasn't watching. He slipped a piece of paper with a message on to me.

"Nothing in this world or any other will keep us apart, Jimmy. You remember that."

I nodded, then he left. I sat holding the piece of paper and staring after him. Then something snapped inside me. I pulled on my trousers and ran for the door. Nan made a grab for me but I wriggled away from her grasp and shot into the street. Barefoot I ran, on and on until I caught sight of him in the distance catching a tram.

"Nothing will keep us apart, Dad," I yelled, repeating his words. "Not in this world or any other."

I saw him turn round. He waved, then he was gone.

♦ ♦ ♦ ♦ ♦

It was as if we'd lost both parents in the bombing. Nan wouldn't have Dad's name mentioned in the house. If me or Molly dared she would give us a back-hander and send us off to bed, no matter what the time. But I had the piece of paper and that was something Nan knew nothing about.

After a few weeks she told us there were going to be changes. Uncle Eddie's house had been bombed so he was going to move in with his family. There was Aunt Lizzie and their children: Lilly, Nelly, Jane, Mary, Ann, John and little Eddie. I knew I was going to get a hiding for it but I argued with Nan.

"They can't move in," I said. "Where will Dad sleep when he comes home?"

"You dare mention that man's name in this house!" she cried. "After what he did."

"Yes, I dare," I shouted back. "He's my dad and that's that."

But that wasn't that. She got hold of the coal shovel and swung it at me until I retreated to bed. Molly stood snivelling until Nan bawled at her to stop. We both cried ourselves to sleep that night. But after Molly dropped off I got Dad's note from a hole in the skirting and read it again. Whenever he was in port a mate of his, Peter Kelly, would get a message to me and I would meet him on the street corner. The note was still in my hand when I woke the next day.

Though there were a lot of them, Eddie and Lizzie's children didn't bother us. For a start, there was a whole new crowd to play with. But there was one person we dreaded seeing in the house. Her name was Marlene Grogan. We never knew where she came from or why she turned up but when they were together, she and Nan acted like the closest friends you could imagine. Marlene wore a heavy shawl and a permanent smile, as though she was simple. But there was one thing about her you never forget. If Nan was partial to a glass of Guinness, Marlene had it flowing in her veins instead of blood. Whenever Marlene showed up she and Nan would go on a bender and spend the next three or four days rotten drunk. They would be up all hours singing sentimental songs and cackling like a pair of witches. Worst of all, Marlene would stagger into our room stinking of booze and sleep in Molly's bed. Marlene had a mouth like a clam. From one end came the stink of ale and from the other a snore that could rattle the ornaments on the mantelpiece.

"Come home, Dad," I would whisper into my pillow before dropping off. "Please come home and take us away."

I lost count of the number of times I had to explain to Molly where Dad had gone.

"He's gone away to sea," I told her.

"Why has he?"

"Because he's got to run the lines…"

"What does that mean?" Molly asked.

"He's trying to bring food to England," I explained. "The Germans are trying to stop him so they can starve us out and win the War. Don't you know anything?"

"More than you," she sniffed and walked away.

I was fed up of explaining. I just wanted Dad to come home so he could tell her himself and shut her up.

My dream came true that Saturday night. I was playing down The Swings when a tall wiry man came along.

"The name's Peter Kelly," he said. "Are you John Byrne's boy?"

My heart skipped a beat.

"Yes."

"Did your dad tell you to expect me?"

"Yes."

Kelly smiled.

"Well, he's home, son. When's the best time to meet him?"

"Nan'll be down the boozer by eight o'clock," I said. "Tell Dad me and Molly will be on the street corner at ten past."

Kelly winked.

"He'll be glad to see you."

Dad didn't let us down. Molly and me were on the corner at five past. He was already there. Molly threw herself into his arms. I waited patiently for my turn.

"Jerry didn't get you then?" I said, trying to sound manly.

Jerry meant the Germans.

Dad shook his head.

"There isn't a U-boat captain living who can catch Johnny Byrne."

He put his hand inside his raincoat.

"Here," he said. "I brought you something."

It looked like a turnip with whiskers.

"What is it?" Molly asked, her eyes widening.

Because of the War, Molly had never seen fruit. I had but I'd all but forgotten what it looked like.

"It's a coconut," Dad said. "You drill a hole in it and drink the milk."

"It gives milk?" I gasped. "Like a cow?"

Dad laughed.

"Not quite. There's white stuff inside the shell too, the pulp. You can eat it."

He drew us closer.

"And when you've finished the inside, you can cut the shell in half and make a sound like horses' hooves."

The coconut tasted amazing and we loved making the sound of horses' hooves. It was almost as loud as the drone of the Heinkels or the thump of the bombs they dropped. We hid the coconut from Nan and she never knew we'd seen Dad. We met him four times before he had to go away again. One day he even took us to his digs.

"A pal lets me stay," he said.

Dad didn't have any family. He went to an orphanage when he was little.

"That's why you have to put up with Kathleen," he said. "Just until this war is over and I can get a job onshore."

Even when Dad was away at sea, things kept him in our minds. Lots of kids were coming back from evacuation in north Wales and school had started again. Molly took her half of the coconut in to show the class. She had a teacher called Miss Humphries.

"Molly," she said. "Have you got any more of that coconut?"

"You can have it," Molly said. "I just want to keep the shell to make a noise like a horse."

Miss Humphries was delighted.

"It's for my little budgie Billy," she said. "He's had nothing like it since the War started."

That made Molly the teacher's pet. She loved Dad even more for that.

The next time Dad came home he had something new. I recognized it immediately. It was a banana. Molly didn't know what to make of it.

"You eat it," Dad said.

Molly gave it a brief lick and grimaced.

"I don't like it," she said.

"Not like that," Dad told her. "You've got to unpeel the skin first."

He showed her how.

"Now try it."

This time Molly stuffed it in.

"So do you like it?" Dad asked.

Molly's eyes were round as saucers and her cheeks were puffed up.

"It's lovely," she said, though it was hard to make out a word she said because of the mouthful of banana.

Before Dad went back to his ship this time he gave us three shillings each.

"Don't let Kathleen find it," he said. "She'll only drink it away."

"Don't worry," I told him. "We're good at hiding things from Nan."

But I couldn't have been more wrong. When we got home that night the gas light was on in the parlour. We thought it was Uncle Eddie and Aunt Lizzie. The moment we walked through the door we saw who it really was.

"Nan!"

"Empty your pockets," she ordered.

"Why?"

"Because I say so."

I tried to be defiant.

"We've got nothing," I told her.

"Empty them out, I say."

Molly was starting to whimper.

"Now look what you've done," I said, trying to change the subject.

Nan wasn't having any.

"Do it," she said.

The moment I emptied my pockets her eyes lit on the six shiny coins.

"You can't have them," Molly cried as Nan reached for them. "He gave them to us."

I saw the hawk look in Nan's eyes.

"Who's he?" she asked.

As if she didn't know.

"I said," Nan insisted, "who is he?"

"You know who," I cried. "Dad."

"You've been seeing him behind my back?" Nan yelled.

"Yes," I shouted back. "And we'll see him again. You see if we don't."

Nan scooped up the coins.

"We'll see about that," she said.

Marlene stayed for the next three nights. Our coins helped to pay for the Guinness.

✝✝✝✝✝

The next time Kelly came to tell me Dad was home, Molly and me took more care than usual. We followed Nan all the way to the pub before we went to see him.

"Dad!"

Molly squealed with delight the moment she saw him turn the corner. As usual I waited my turn. We told Dad about the money. His eyes narrowed.

"The war won't last much longer," he said darkly, as if he knew Mr Churchill personally. "Then I'll take you away from her for good."

The words were barely out of his mouth when we heard a familiar voice.

"I knew you were sneaking around," Nan said. "Turning up handing out your blood money as if it will make up for what you did."

"I did nothing," Dad said. "It was the bombs took your daughter, Kathleen. Your daughter and *my wife*."

That did it. Nan flew at him, punching him and slapping him round the face. Dad didn't do a thing. He just stood there taking it. Molly was screaming and crying, begging Nan to stop.

"Oh, I'll stop," said Nan. "I'll stop when he says he's never coming back."

She was panting from all the shouting.

"Don't you come near these kids again," she screamed as he walked away. "Ever!"

I know why Dad walked away. He had nowhere to take us. She'd won.

By then the bombing had stopped but Dad still had to run the lines. No matter what Nan said, we still found ways to see him when he came home.

Then one day Peter Kelly caught up with me on Titchfield Street.

"I didn't expect him back so soon," I said.

I saw Kelly's face change. My insides turned over.

"What's wrong?"

"It's the ship, lad. It's reported missing. It was a torpedo."

"Oh no. No!"

I waited a beat.

"Survivors?"

Kelly shook his head.

"There's no word, son. I'm sorry."

There was only one thing left to say.

"What do I tell Molly?"

👫👫👫

That night Molly sobbed and sobbed. I wanted to join her but I knew I couldn't. I had to keep up appearances. I put my arms round Molly though she was nearly ten by then. I rocked her and told it would be all right.

"You heard what Dad told us that time," I said. "There's not a U-boat captain living that can catch John Byrne."

Molly looked at me through her tears.

"You really think so?"

Though my throat was choked with sobs, I kept up the brave face.

"I know it, Moll."

I became aware of Nan watching from the doorway. Even she didn't dare say anything that night.

"Remember what he said? Nothing will keep us apart in this world or any other."

Molly fell asleep that night murmuring the words. I didn't have the heart to tell her I knew it was a fairy tale.

*♦♦♦♦♦*

Weeks went by. Though I knew it was hopeless I imagined the day Peter Kelly would come looking for me and tell me Dad was home. Months went by. Soon I stopped believing he was coming back, even in my wildest dreams. But I pretended, for Molly's sake, and to keep up appearances. What's more, I wasn't going to let Nan think she'd won.

"He's coming back," I kept telling her. "Even if it's just to spite you."

I was fourteen by then and nothing Nan did could frighten me any more. She could scream and shout, she could shake her fist, she could swing the coal shovel, but nothing did any good. I just stared back and told her I wasn't scared. One night I won my first real battle. I heard her come through the door with Marlene Grogan. I saw the look on Molly's face as Marlene staggered towards her bed. That's when I made up my mind.

"You can stop right there," I said.

Marlene stood rocking.

"What's going on?" Nan demanded, her voice thick with drink.

"He won't let me in my room," Marlene said.

"It's not your room," I told her. "And it's not your bed. If you want a bed, you can share with her."

I pointed at Nan.

"That's a fine way to talk," Nan said. "After I've brought you up."

She reached for the coal shovel but I got there first.

"Want this?" I said. "You can have it if you like."

I waved it in front of her nose.

"You hit my dad once," I said. "And he let you because he's a gentleman. But believe me, Nan, I'm not."

Nan stared for a moment then turned on her heel.

"Come on Marlene," she said.

"Would you have hit her?" Molly asked.

"Of course not," I answered, putting down the shovel. "I'm like my dad, a gentleman."

⁂

I was nearly fifteen when the War ended. There were celebrations in front of St George's Hall. By the time I got there with Molly and a few friends there were thousands of people dancing, cheering, shouting. Some of the soldiers were on top of the lion statues waving their arms.

"Hard to credit it," somebody said.

I turned round. It was Peter Kelly. I hadn't seen him for such a long time. He looked different – greyer and thinner.

"Six years and now it's over," he said.

He had a grin from ear to ear. I thought it was because he'd been drinking, or just because the war was over. Then there was another familiar voice.

"Dad!"

Molly screamed so loud half the heads in the crowd seemed to turn our way.

"Dad!"

He swung her round and round. As usual I waited my turn. Dad looked me up and down.

"It's been a while," he said.

He reached out a hand and we shook. It was his way of saying I wasn't a boy any more. I was a man. I already knew that, because of the way I stood up to Nan.

"What happened to you?" I asked.

Dad drew us to one side and told his tale, how a handful of men made it to the shore. They were taken in by the Norwegian resistance and sat out the War. He tried to get a message to us but had no idea if we had got it. When he finished his story he hugged both of us.

"Does this mean you've come for us?" Molly

asked. "We don't have to go back to Nan's?"

Dad nodded.

"I've got your things."

"Didn't Nan try to stop you?"

Dad winked.

"She tried."

"You didn't hurt her?" Molly said, still scared of the hawk woman.

"Of course not," Dad said, his eyes twinkling. "I'm a gentleman."

Then, voice thick with emotion, he said one last thing before we headed for the tram.

"I told you nothing could keep us apart."

All three of us finished the sentence.

"In this world or any other."

# Handheld

## Daniel Ehrenhaft

*From: Sam Fishman   Time: 10:07 a.m.*
*Subject: running late*

dad. i'm really sorry but there's a problem. the dry cleaner said that my suit isn't ready. if i hang out here they said they might be able to get the stain out in time. tomato sauce is hard to get out. plus there's the red wine on the shoulder. remember? you spilled it on me when you were dancing to that disco song at isaac's bar mitzvah? but you said you had to much wine anyway, so it was okay you spilled it, because then you wouldn't be able to finish the glass. i tried to call from the pay phone here but it was busy. ill try the coffee shop next door. sam.

*Sent from my Wireless Handheld*


*From: Jerry Fishman  Time: 10:10 a.m.*
*Subject: re: running late*

Sam: Thanks for the message. I'll call the dry cleaner. Please go back there if you haven't already. In a worst-case scenario, you can borrow one of Isaac's old suits. You need to be dressed and ready to go soon.

The car is coming at 11. Also…*sigh*… I feel like an ogre for bringing this up right now, but to repeat my overused mantra: THINK BEFORE YOU WRITE. Don't allow this wireless handheld to destroy your grammar. If only to make your nitpicky father happy, could you please try to compose your emails as if you were writing a real letter? Capitalize your sentences. Capitalize the personal pronoun "I". Spell "too" properly. Remember your contractions. Okay – I'll leave you alone now. If your suit isn't ready in the next ten minutes, come home immediately.

Dad

PS I'm pretty sure we got the wine stain out with Spray-and-Wash, yes?

*From: Sam Fishman  Time: 10:15 a.m.*
*Subject: my dad has officially gone insane*

max: check out this email from my dad. i told you he was losing it. don't you think it's weird? it's my grandpa's funeral today and dad is ragging on me about grammar. my therapist says there's a word for that. i can't remember what it is because sometimes i zone out when she talks. but it's when you bug somebody about something stupid, and you do it to ignore what's really bothering you. like, dad is really worried about my grammar? he's going to bury HIS dad today. he should be sad. plus isaac's like 50 times bigger than me so the only suit that will even fit me was a suit from when he was 7 years old and prolly has old chocolate bars in it and smells.

PS: what does mantra mean? that's like zen buddist type stuff right? (FWD: ATTACHED)

*Sent from my Wireless Handheld*


*From: Max Gold Time: 10:22 a.m.*
*Subject: re: my dad has officially gone insane*

dude, dude, dude!!! U are a FREAK. it's a good thing U see a therapist now too cuz you need professional help even more than i do!!!!!!!!!!!

here's what U need to know:

1) "prolly" is lame. only chicks use "prolly".

2) your dad just knows that you're dreading your grandpa's funeral. i bet he thinks you're lying about the suit not being ready.

3) are U lying about the suit? U can tell me, I swear I won't tell.

4) the word your shrink was using is "transference". (i think so anyway). a good example of "transference" would be a twelve-year-old freak lying to his dad pretending his suit wasn't ready so he could skip his grandpa's funeral.

5) HA! HA! HA! LOL... LOL... I really do crack myself up sometimes.

6) please don't tell me you're still reading this on your handheld. and why did your dad buy you that thing anyway? wouldn't a cell phone be easier? maybe he

190

should see a therapist too……..

7) oh yeah and what am i like your personal dictionary slave? Btw- it's "Buddhist" not "buddist".

8) but seriously i am sorry about your grandpa. but he was like totally senile dying for years anyway right? so it's one of those blessing-in-disguise type things right? sorry that came out much harsher than i meant.

9) isaac is a big fat jerk and thinks he's way cooler than he is. i mean he's your brother and all but whatever. sorry that came out much harsher than i meant too.

10) don't wear one of his old suits tho. that would be a new low.

11) Think before you write!!!!!!!!! Just kidding.

*From: Sam Fishman  Time: 10:31 a.m.*
*Subject: re: re: my dad has officially gone insane*

max: you're the freak. it took me like ten minutes to read your email because the screen on this thing is so small. my suit still isn't ready. I wish I had a cell phone. I don't have any change left for the pay phone because I bought some gum. dad bought me this stupid wireless handheld because he hates cell phones. he refuses to buy me or isaac one. he thinks that people only use cell phones to attract attention to themselves. so they can be all like "oh look how important I am!!! I'm getting all these calls, and talking really loud in public, and annoying people, so I must be popular!!!" he actually said that.

*Sent from my Wireless Handheld*

*From: Max Gold  Time: 10:33 a.m.*
*Subject: re: re: re: my dad has officially gone insane*

**dude I hate to bring up the obvious what does any of this have to do with your grandpa's funeral?**

*From: Sam Fishman  Time: 10:34 a.m.*
*Subject: re: re: re: re: my dad has officially gone insane*

**it's "transference".  Ha ha ha LOL LOL… I crack myself up sometimes.**

*Sent from my Wireless Handheld*

*From: Max Gold  Time: 10:35 a.m.*
*Subject: re: re: re: re: re: my dad has officially gone insane*

**do you want to borrow one of MY suits?**

*From: Sam Fishman  Time: 10:37 a.m.*
*Subject: new development!!!*

**ok here's the thing, and I swear I am not making this up. This girl just came in to pick up something from the drycleaners and it wasn't ready and she left her wallet in the seat next to me. now i have it and i'm not sure what to do. maybe I should chase after her.**

*Sent from my Wireless Handheld*

*From: Max Gold  Time: 10:38 a.m.*
*Subject: re: new development!!!*

**U are such a liar. i bet you're not even in the**

drycleaner's right now! you're at the coffee shop just making all this stuff up. and if your dad catches U, I'll be your alibi. So U can be like: "oh no, dad, I was at the drycleaner's waiting for my suit! and it wasn't ready! and I found this girl's wallet! so i had to chase after her! so i couldn't go to grandpa's funeral! U can ask Max! I talked to him the whole time! I swear!"

*From: Sam Fishman  Time: 10:40 a.m.*
*Subject: re: re: new development!!!*

max are you on drugs? Where do you get this from? I swear I'm at the drycleaners. you live 5 minutes away. you want to come check for yourself? but i feel creepy looking through some girl's wallet who i don't know. and now that weird cashier guy is looking at me even tho he's on the phone. cuz i've been sitting here typing on this wireless handheld for like 25 minutes. even tho he should be sorry! cuz my suit isn't ready and it's my GRANDPA'S FUNERAL!!!
*Sent from my Wireless Handheld*

*From: Max Gold  Time: 10:42 a.m.*
*Subject: re: re: re: new development!!!*

ok ok…dude get a grip. don't lose it on me. U are gonna be 13 yrs old in 3 months. that's an adult man according to the laws of jewishness. so suck it up and look thru the wallet and get home as soon as U can. cuz if your dad finds out you've been talking to me all this time he's gonna be pissed cuz he hates me.

btw- mantra means a trap for catching poachers

*From: Sam Fishman  Time: 10:43 a.m.*
*Subject: re: re: re: re: new development!!!*

max, my dad doesn't hate you. he just thinks you're weird, which you are. are you sure that's what mantra means? anyway you'll be proud of me. i looked through the wallet and it belongs to this girl named melody otis. she looks familiar actually. did she go to our school? she's got curly black hair. the address is pretty near here so i think I'm gonna drop it off...my suit's still not ready....

*Sent from my Wireless Handheld*

*From: Max Gold Time: 10:44 a.m.*
*Subject: re: re: re: re: re: new development!!!*

melody otis???? DUDE! DUUUUUUUDE! she is like the hottest hottie on the planet! she's in 10th grade now... kirk otis is her brother...that little wiener in the 5th grade who does the card tricks....OK dude you have to parlay this into something good. btwn U and me this is massive!!! MASSIVE...How about this? I'll come meet U and U give me the wallet and I'll give it to Melody.

*From: Sam Fishman   Time: 10:45 a.m.*
*Subject: Too Late*

i just gave the wallet to the cashier guy and he sez my suit
will be ready in 5 minutes. He's calling melody right now. sorry.
*Sent from my Wireless Handheld*


*From: Jerry Fishman   Time: 10:46 a.m.*
*Subject: re: running late*

Sam, what is going on? The car service is picking
us up in fifteen minutes. I've called the drycleaner
several times, but the line is busy. Is your suit ready?  I
sent you on this simple errand because I believed that
you were mature enough to run it. I understand that
these are difficult circumstances, but I must say: I'm
concerned. Do you need me to come over there and
handle this myself?


*From: Sam Fishman   Time: 10:47 a.m.*
*Subject: re: re: running late*

Dad, I'm really sorry. The suit is almost ready. I'll be
home soon.
*Sent from my Wireless Handheld*


*From: Jerry Fishman   Time: 10:48 a.m.*
*Subject: re: re: re: running late*

You know what? Don't bother. If you don't want to
come to Grandpa's funeral, fine. I understand. He had

very few marbles rolling around upstairs for most of your life. He made you uncomfortable whenever he pinched your cheek or called you by another name. Nursing homes are not the most pleasant places to visit. But you should have skipped visiting him there instead of skipping out on him here. I just wish you'd talked to me about this first. Please don't lie and hide from me. Isaac and I are leaving.

*From: Sam Fishman Time: 10:50 a.m.*
*Subject: fwd: re: re: re: running late*

ok Max, just 1 more thing: check out this email........Now: you know why my dad really gave me this freaking wireless handheld? He gave it to me so he won't have to talk to me. That's why he didn't buy me a cell phone. If he bought me a cell phone then we'd actually have to talk. He doesn't know how. I'M NOT KIDDING. HE NEVER EVER TALKED TO ME ABOUT THE NURSING HOME. HE JUST FORCED ME TO GO. MY THERAPIST SAYS THERE'S A WORD FOR TALKING-WITHOUT-TALKING TOO AND I CAN'T REMEMBER THAT EITHER. (FWD: ATTACHED)
*Sent from my Wireless Handheld*

*From: Max Gold Time: 10:54 a.m.*
*Subject: re: re: re: re: running late*

ok...ok...just chill. what's with the all caps? are U that upset? U are freaking me out! seriously, take a deep breath. U want to see something that'll make U feel better about how weird your dad is? my mom makes your dad look like the sanest person on the planet. See…U know how i hate going to my piano lesson? cuz my teacher's house smells like dog pee? well, today I lied and this is the email exchange my mom and I had:

BEGIN FORWARDED MESSAGE------------

Hi Mom…Listen, sorry to spring this on you at the last minute, but Sam is in a bit of a jam. He's at the drycleaners and his suit isn't ready. He needs to borrow a suit for his grandfather's funeral because his Dad spilled wine on his…anyway, to make a long story short: Can you call Mrs Rubin and ask her if I can reschedule? I'm running to meet him now at the drycleaners. Thanks!

Love, Max


*From: Shirley Gold  Time: 10:48 a.m.*
*Subject: re: re: re: re: running late*

Max! Karma! No need to worry about Mrs Rubin; she called me at work to reschedule! Her Wheaton Terrier, Agnes, just gave birth! 7 smelly puppies! Lucky for you: No piano lessons for at least another couple of weeks! :-)! Hopefully, this will serve as motivation for Mrs Rubin to disinfect her music room and eliminate the foul odor, as well!  So anyway, I invited Aunt Gretchen to come over to spend time with you! She can walk you to the dry cleaners!

You know how she loves walks! You are very sweet to try to catch up with your friend Sam! If you don't catch up with him, however, I suggest you drop off your own suit at the drycleaners! It could also use some help in the odor department!  :-)!

Love, Mom!

END FORWARDED MESSAGE-----------

the exclamation points speak for themselves, wouldn't you say? my mom didn't forget jack either. she just wants my aunt to watch me to make sure i don't get in trouble. anyway my point is: your dad is just really messed up right now. also my aunt can lend U the money to take a cab to the cemetery. I'm going to walk her to the dry cleaners. she likes to go on walks.

PS: I accidentally told U the definition for "mantrap" which is right below "mantra" in the dictionary. "mantra" is a word or sound repeated to aid in concentration or meditation in Hinduism or Buddhism. karma's a word like that too.

PPS: we're leaving right now. I'll text U on my celly.

PPPS: Can U give me Melody's digits?

*From: Sam Fishman  Time: 10:59 a.m.*
*Subject: re: re: re: re: re: running late*

thanxs. that email took me even longer to read than the first one you sent. And i'm not that upset or angry. i accidentally hit the caps button. Seriously. but thanx.

gretchen is your deaf aunt right? i feel weird about borrowing money from her.

*Sent from my Wireless Handheld*

*From: Max Gold  Time: 11:00 a.m.*
*Subject: gretchen*

U feel weird cuz she's deaf? i think she's over it dude. she's been deaf her whole life. also, "thanx" is even lamer than "prolly". And there IS no caps button on a wireless.

*From: Sam Fishman  Time: 11:02 a.m.*
*Subject: re: gretchen*

not because she's deaf you putz. cuz she's a grown-up. and there is a caps button. At least I'm pretty sure there is.

*Sent from my Wireless Handheld*

*From: Max Gold  Time: 11:02 a.m.*
*Subject: re: re: gretchen*

gretchen's cool dude. u met her.  anyway, she just got here and i explained the whole situation. see u in 5. what about melody's digits?

*From: Sam Fishman  Time: 11:02 a.m.*
*Subject: re: re: re: gretchen*

are you sure Gretchen is cool with it? I really appreciate it. I don't have melody's digits. besides you're a 12-year-old dork and she's a 16-year-old hottie so

there's no hope. And there's one more thing… you'll see,
I'm not at the drycleaner's—

*Sent from my Wireless Handheld*

*From: Max Gold  Time: 11:02 a.m.*
*Subject: re: re: re: re: gretchen*

dude why are u even still texting me we're like
10 feet away… oh my god dude you're in the coffee
shop. i see u in the window! u liar! i knew it!

*From: Jerry Fishman  Time: 11:05 a.m.*
*Subject: re: re: re: running late*

Sam: I hope you get this. I am sorry for exploding
and accusing you of lying. Please come home right
now. The car is here. Isaac and I will wait another
fifteen minutes. I'll try the drycleaner's again, too. I
think the phone is broken.

Love, Dad

*From: Sam Fishman  Time: 11:07 a.m.*
*Subject: re: re: re: re: running late*

Dad: The phone at the drycleaner's is indeed broken.
I've known that all along. But good news! The suit is
ready.  Max came to help out and his aunt lent me some
money, so I am taking a cab. I'm changing here and I will
see you there. Go on ahead. I don't want to make you
late. Okay? I promise I'll be there. Can I ask you a favour,

though? Can I throw out the wireless handheld? It's a pain in the butt and my fingers hurt. Sam

*Sent from my Wireless Handheld*

*From: Jerry Fishman  Time: 11:07 a.m.*
*Subject: re: re: re: re: re: running late*

sam, honestly you can do whatever you like, so long as i see you at the funeral. you know how to get to the cemetery, yes? please thank Max's aunt for me......we'll reimburse her ASAP....running out the door........love.....

*From: Sam Fishman  Time: 11:02 am*
*Subject: talking*

Dad: Got it. I hope you get this, too. Nice grammar, btw. Ha! So you know, even without the wireless handheld, I figured out a new way we can still talk without talking. We can learn sign language! Seriously! There are whole different rules of grammar, too! See, just now, I saw Max get in a fight with his aunt. You know how she's deaf? Anyway, the fight was about how Max wants to go stalk some girl named Melody, and also about how Gretchen was pretty ticked off because she lent me cab fare when my suit was ready the whole time – because, yes: I lied, and I hid at the coffee shop next door (but then Gretchen laughed because I really DID find this girl Melody's wallet) – and it was pretty cool to watch Max and Gretchen fight and laugh and make up, all by waving their hands, and then holding them at the end, even if they attracted a lot of attention.

Sam

*Sent from my Wireless Handheld*

# Begi-Begi and Jill-Jillie

## Farrukh Dhondy

Dad disappeared when I was seven. My mum said he treated us cruelly and my sister and I could see that she worked very hard, cleaning people's houses, looking after other people's children during the day and sometimes baby-sitting them into the night. The flat was always noisy with the sound of crying babies. My little sister may have forgotten our dad, but for me he was always there. I could see his hands, feel his presence. He was gone, of course. He had left us, but secretly, without ever saying it to Mum or to Sonia my sister, I felt, as if by magic, he was with us.

You see, Dad was a magician. A real one. But he was strange because he said he didn't believe in magic. Like God; who doesn't believe in God? He used to show me, when we were only five and four years old, how to do a few tricks myself. He did this trick of the 'two-headed-coin'. You hold a pound coin in your right hand and show your audience that it's heads up. Then you slap it onto your left hand and move your right hand away and it's still heads. It hasn't flipped over. My friends are still intrigued by the trick and try and grab the coin to see if it's really a coin with two heads. Of course it isn't. You have to learn the trick of letting the coin fall under its own weight and not be twisted by your turning hand.

He always said he wanted me to grow up to be a scientist so he'd show me tricks, which he could explain with science, like balancing two forks on the edge of a glass by hanging them on a fifty pence piece. It looks like magic but it isn't. And he used to tell me that all magic had its explanations. The audience mustn't be told that, and it would spoil the fun to tell me how the tricks worked, but that I was family and within the family we had to know that there was no such thing as magic.

At my seventh birthday party he did some very good tricks. We lived in a house with a garden and I invited my friends from school and Dad gave them a magic show. He was doing shows all over the country then and his assistant Clara used to sit in the box and be cut in two. She came to the party too and they weren't going to do that trick at all, but then my sister, who was five, kept shouting, "Cut Clara up, cut Clara up," and when I told my friends what she was saying they crowded round my dad and asked him if he could cut the lady in two. He did. Clara got changed into her costume which was kept in our magic garage and they brought the box out and turned on the music tape and everyone was amazed when she came out in one piece, dancing.

Dad did the snake trick, letting his snakes out of the jar and making them disappear when all the kids screamed and scrambled. The snakes slithered out of the jar and the kids started to run out when my dad asked them what they were frightened of and they said the snakes.

"Where? What snakes?" he said and when we looked the snakes were all in the jar again. They all thought that was so cool.

He used to say, "Begi-begi and jill-jillie," before making things appear or disappear. It was the spell he used.

"Why don't you say 'abracadabra', like other magicians?" I asked him.

"Because the power of 'begi-begi' is much greater than the power of 'abracadabra'. It's older and stronger and more mysterious," he said.

So that was the spell I used at nights, kneeling by my bed and praying with all my might to the powers that made magic work, to try and get him back. Just after he went missing my mum told us that he was on tour and he would be coming back. We were used to his being away for a few days and even for a week or two when it was a long engagement at the seaside in summer. But this time he didn't come back and it became clear to me that he didn't intend to return home and to us. He must have phoned Mum or told her and I knew she missed him and wanted him back, but she didn't want to show us that she was sad.

I don't know how long it was after he left that she told us that Dad had gone back to India, that he still loved us but he wanted to be on his own to think things out. I didn't understand what she meant. What I imagined was Dad climbing a bare mountain with a bundle on his back, quite alone with no one for miles and miles around, walking and 'thinking things out'.

After he'd gone we stopped hopping from town to town and from flat to flat like we had before. I remember moving in those days, before I was seven, from London, to Swindon, to Glasgow and other places I don't remember. We moved, my mum said, because Dad had to get work in different places. My mum moved my sister and me from school to school. Now that he was gone there was no need to pack our raggy bags and move every few months. We stayed put and Mum went to work or brought kids in for minding.

When we were 'on the road', as my father called it, he would get dressed up in silk suits and Indian scarves and things to do his stuff. He called himself The Great Varuna, which, he told us, was the God of

Thunder. Sometimes we'd go and watch him perform. I was so proud of him, being able to do things that left other people standing, gaping, wondering, amazed.

I thought my dad was terrific. I didn't stop to think then that it wasn't much of a life for my mum. I didn't realize that she needed him even more than we did. Oh, I knew she cried. We never heard them fight or argue, but when he left the house she would cry and wash her face to hide her tears. But we knew because her eyes would turn blotchy and her face would puff up.

When I was very young, from when I can remember, we moved from town to town, changing houses and schools. Finally, in the last year Dad was with us, we settled down in a flat in Greenford in London. It was only two rooms and a kitchen. My sister and I went to a new school. My dad had a job touring several theatres with a company of performers. His magic act was, at the time, lacking an assistant, because the girl who used to work for him had got fed up of travelling. Dad said she'd found a boyfriend and gone and that she couldn't be replaced because she was worth her weight in gold. She didn't look very heavy to me. Now his act had a rabbit which, during the act, he used to pull out of his big red turban. Dad said it was our job to look after it.

The rabbit was called Saffy. It was actually called 'safaid' which, Dad explained, means 'white' in India – but we called it 'Saffy'.

Mum said we had settled down in Greenford and told us that she wanted us to stay in the same school now that we were six and seven. Dad would spend some nights away and on other nights when he was working near or in London, he would come home after midnight and unpack his stuff and sometimes I would wake up and hear him talking softly to the rabbit as he put him in his cage.

Then, a few months after we got him, poor Saffy got the sniffles. My father, Sonia and I took him to the vet who said he had a sort of rabbit flu and that's why his eyes had got red and his nose was leaking and had begun to get brown and crusty round the edge of the nostrils. She gave us some rabbit pills and asked us if we had any other pets, because he had to be kept away from them or they would get sick too.

That was bad. My father was working then in a small circus. He was supposed to go on tour with it and he wasn't allowed to take Saffy with him because there would be other animals there and the circus manager didn't want a sick and infectious rabbit on their travels.

We were very happy. We'd look after Saffy ourselves while Dad was away. So we kept him in his cage and every evening after school we'd shut the kitchen door and let him out and at weekends we took him down to the common where there were some bushes and let him loose and then spent hours sometimes trying to catch him again, because he used to run away and crouch in hiding places in the foliage.

When my father came back from the circus tour, Saffy seemed much better. We'd take the gunge off his nostrils with cotton wool and hot water every day and apply the cream the vet gave us to his twitching nose.

My mother had been to our school that week and, maybe because she wanted to show off, she told the Headmistress that our dad was a magician and that he would come before the Christmas break and entertain the school for nothing. My father said there was another tour and he had to go back to the circus after a rest, but sure, he'd do a show for our school.

I really wanted him to. Some of the other boys in my school talked about their fathers. Some had shops and sold groceries. Some of them worked for the railway as drivers and ticket collectors. One boy's father was a photographer, but no one's father was anything as intriguing as a magician. The other kids asked me about it, the boys and the girls, and they imagined all sorts of weird things.

"Is your dad haunted?" one kid asked me.

"Does he get his powers from the devil?" another one said.

I said he was just very clever and could make things appear and disappear and now, even those who didn't believe me, would see for themselves. I didn't want to tell them that magic wasn't really magic. That was our secret.

My dad knew I was just waiting for the day of the great performance, when The Great Varuna would bring his magical thunder to our little school stage. Even the teachers began asking me about Dad's magical powers. He was a man of mystery. They hadn't seen him because he never came to the school gates to drop us off or pick us up. He was always on tour or resting from a tour or working in the locked front room, drawing diagrams and making measurements which I thought went into the spells for the new magic.

Then the day of the show arrived and our teacher made us arrange the stage and put out the mats for the children to sit on. I was proud to take charge.

"Will your dad require any chairs on stage or anything?" the teacher asked.

"He said two jugs of water, which he'll bring himself, and a tablecloth for the table. He'll bring that too. He carries everything he needs," I said.

The one thing I was hoping was that he wouldn't park his big old car in front of the school. It wasn't smart. It was maroon coloured, its bumpers had fallen off and the wheels were all black and dirty. It was funny, but I had never thought about the state of the car before that. It was just Dad's old banger — the magic carpet, he called it.

But he did park the car right in front of the school and he asked the school keeper's assistant to give him a hand with all the stuff he had to carry onto stage.

We were in the playground when he arrived and all the kids went to the fence to watch him come in. He was dressed in his trousers and shirt and he carried his battered old suitcase with its gowns and magician's costumes in it. He waved to me and smiled at the other kids who gathered round him.

"Is that your dad?" they asked.

Some of the bolder kids gathered round him and walked with him asking what the props and stuff were. He was carrying Saffy's cage with a drape over it so no one could see it was a rabbit. He paused and pulled coins out of a boy's nose.

"They didn't come out of his nose," another kid said.

"You saw it," my dad said.

"He's snotty and the pounds would be full of snot from his nose," the cheeky kid said.

After the break we all filed into the hall and sat on the mats.

"Stay away from the radiator cages," Mr K, our

teacher, shouted when some of the kids started rattling the metal cages that were fixed over the central heating radiators in our school hall. The usual disruption was to take a ruler and drag it down stiff over the cage to make a racket, and when ten kids did it at the same time it sounded really horrible.

Then the show started and there was a sudden hush. Dad came on in a blue silk gown with the signs of the Zodiac on it − moons and stars and a few reverse-Swastika signs.

"Is your dad a Nazi?" the kid next to me asked.

"They're not Nazi Swastikas. Those are anti-clockwise. These are clockwise and they are ancient Indian signs for good luck," I said.

It was what my father had told me and I would have thought the other Indian kids in the school, and there were quite a few, would have known that.

He introduced himself as The Great Varuna and told the kids he had to have his lunch and then he started swallowing a long string of coloured scarves knotted together. He must have eaten fifteen of them tied together. The whole school laughed and then Dad opened his mouth and the scarves were gone. Empty mouth. He'd swallowed them.

"You ate them!" a little girl from Year 2 in the front row shouted.

Dad smiled and pulled the scarves out of his

mouth one by one. They were not knotted now and he fluttered each of them, as they emerged from his mouth, crisp and dry and ironed. He got a huge clap and I knew I was grinning with pride.

I could see he wanted an even bigger clap and he asked Mr Bulford, the teacher who was standing by the stage, for his watch. The teacher took off his watch and gave it to Dad, who put it on a sheet of metal and smashed it to bits with a big hammer. The kids all gasped and the little girl stood up and shouted, "That's naughty, that's naughty".

Dad showed the front row of kids the bits and then he flung them out of an open window.

Bully, which is what we all called Mr Bulford, grinned foolishly.

"Takes the weight off your wrist, doesn't it?" Dad asked him.

"That is a very expensive watch," Bully said.

"You mean it was a very expensive watch?" Dad said.

The kids didn't know whether to laugh or not because everyone was scared of Bully-boy who was very strict. Dad didn't keep the kids in suspense much longer. He turned to a boy in the front row.

"Now why have you stolen your teacher's watch?" he asked.

The boy looked puzzled.

"Get it out of your pocket," Dad said and the boy

dipped into his pocket and there was the watch. He pulled it out. He couldn't believe his eyes. He gave it back to Bully.

"You must teach them not to steal watches," Dad said, and everyone clapped loud and long.

Dad did a few more tricks. He gave four kids in the front row sheets of paper and crayons and asked them to draw quick pictures. He took the pictures and held them up and then he shuffled them in front of our eyes, turned them round once and twice and showed us the sheets of paper, and the drawings had disappeared. He handed the sheets round again. There was nothing on them. He asked the same children to do another drawing quickly or write their names in crayon. Then he took the sheets of paper and held them up and when he turned them round the drawings they had first done were back again.

"How weird is that. Your dad's cool, guy," the boy who had asked about the Nazi sign said.

It was all going too well. Dad picked up the red silk hat and showed it to the audience. It was empty. Then he put his hand in and pulled Saffy out of it. The girls all went 'Aww', and the girl in front said, 'Tweet lickle wabbit', and everyone laughed.

But Saffy looked a bit miserable and I could see that the thing on his nostrils had started again because they were dry and scabby. Maybe no one else could see that, but I was thinking Dad should have avoided this trick and done something else. After all he had worked his magic without Saffy for two weeks. He didn't have to bring him along.

Then he made him disappear again. He covered up the hat with a black cloth and put the hat on the table. The cloth jumped up and down, showing that Saffy was still in there dancing about. Then he took the cloth away and the rabbit wasn't in the hat which Dad passed around to show people that it didn't have a false bottom or top or whatever.

"Where did it go?" the girl in the front row said, turning round and looking at the rest of the audience with a raised hand.

And then, just as Dad was stooping to take the hat back, a button or fastening snapped in the fold of his silk gown and the gown fell open. Saffy, white and sniffing now with a faint sound, which sounded very loud in the silent hall, fell out of the gown and scrambled to his feet in the hall. Dad scrambled to shut the flap in his silken gown. Before he did, the audience could see that he had long johns on underneath with pockets and straps and buckles of all sorts. Or perhaps they hadn't noticed that as I had. Perhaps they were looking at the rabbit.

"There he is!" said the little commentating girl.

I'll never forget the startled look on Dad's face. I

held my breath. He would pass it off as an intentional joke, part of the magic. How did the rabbit get from the hat to a pouch in his long johns?

But for once my father, The Great Varuna, slipped. He got down and tried to grab Saffy who hopped away from him into the audience. Instead of letting him go, Dad scrambled through the audience after him. The whole hall laughed. And again I saw Dad's eyes. For the first time in my life I saw panic in them. I had never seen panic in anyone's eyes before.

Saffy ran into one of the radiator cages and found a gap below one and crawled in.

"The radiators are boiling hot, he'll get roasted," Mr K shouted and Dad was on his hands and knees groping to grab Saffy from under the cage. I was standing up and desperately watching the magic aura around my father melt away.

Dad struggled to pull Saffy out from under the metal wire of the cage and Saffy struggled to get away. He finally pulled him out and as he did it, the wire cut his forearm and made it bleed. Dad stood up, holding the rabbit and looking confused. Drops of blood began to fall from his forearm and then, in another separate flow, from below Saffy's belly. There was a boy sitting next to the cage and the drops of blood fell on him and he raised his arm and stood up.

"His willy is bleeding. The rabbit's willy," the

boy shouted.

The whole hall went wild. Bully and the headmistress came to the front of the hall, and Dad just stood there holding the bleeding rabbit as though he didn't quite know what had happened. I looked at him and I should never have seen that. It was seeing my father without anything with which to fight the world. It was like seeing him without any clothes on. My heart beat faster and felt as though it was sinking inside me.

It seemed to me that Dad stood like that for a long time, but it may only have been one second. And just like Dad, he tried to make a joke of it.

"No-one escapes The Great Varuna," he said. "Don't worry about the blood. It only looks like he's bleeding. Seeing is deceiving."

He went back and climbed the three steps leading to the stage but the headmistress who had rushed to the front of the hall by then said, "No, no, Mr Varuna, I can clearly see he really is bleeding. You had better do something. School, quiet! The show's over. Thank you, Mr Varuna. We need to find a bandage for that animal."

She went up to him and tried to take the bleeding rabbit from his hands but Dad held on to it and pulled Saffy away. The headmistress's hands came away all bloody.

"Leave him to me," Dad was shouting.

I didn't hear or see any more. I shot out of the hall. The gate was shut and locked but we knew how to get out of school through the hedge and I was out and away. I ran home.

Sonia came back at home time. I couldn't bring myself to tell my mum what had happened at school. I couldn't tell her that I never wanted to go back to that school again. She kept asking me why I had come home, about the show and about Dad, but I wouldn't say a word. I couldn't. Sonia came home and I told her the whole story so she knew all about it when Dad came back.

Dad came home after dinnertime. He had been in the pub drinking and the alcohol was on his breath. He tried to act normal and started unloading his equipment from the back of the car and bringing it up the stairs in stages. The last thing he brought up was Saffy in his cage. The cage still had the drape over it.

He went to the kitchen and took out a bottle of brandy he kept there. Mum went in and took it from him. Meanwhile Sonia lifted the drape on Saffy's cage. The white rabbit was crouching in a pool of blood and breathing hard.

"Dad, get the vet. Take him to the vet," I shouted and both Mum and Dad came out of the kitchen. Mum took one look at Saffy and held her face in horror.

Dad stepped up to the cage, dropped the drape

and took the cage into the kitchen.

He shut the kitchen door behind him.

"No, Dad. No, you can't!" I shouted and tried to get into the kitchen but he had bolted it on the other side. He didn't say anything. Both Sonia and I banged the door until our fists were blue. My mum sat on the sofa, tears down her cheeks.

We heard the taps of the sink turn on in a gush and the pipes in the whole flat began to hum. We carried on pounding the door. I don't know if Sonia knew why we were banging it, but I certainly did.

After a minute or perhaps it was more, my dad unbolted the door and came out of the kitchen with a plastic carrier bag with the limp, long weight in it. He walked out of the front door.

In the kitchen the cage was open on the floor and still bloody. Mum followed us in and started wetting the sponges to clean it up. In the sink there was the bread knife with blood on it.

My dad returned late at night when we were all in bed. We weren't asleep. Sonia and I slept in the front room on the sofa bed when dad was home and Mum and Dad slept in the bedroom.

"I've buried him," he said to us. "No magic could save him. That boy was right. He had ripped something under his belly and he was bleeding to death. Sometimes you have to do what seems cruel."

I wasn't listening to that.

"It was cruel," I said. "You are cruel. You should have taken him to the vet."

"I don't have money for animal operations," my father said.

"And you are a useless magician," I said. "You showed me up."

My father didn't reply.

"And... and you... you're not magician at all. Not like a real one."

I shouldn't have said that and I knew I shouldn't have as soon as I had said it. My dad didn't even look in my face. He turned and went into the bedroom and shut the door. For a long time we heard him arguing with my mother, fighting, trying to keep their voices down – as though we couldn't hear.

I didn't see my father for a few days after that. Mum said he was on tour again, but when he came back he said he had found work in Southall in a shoe shop. We never discussed why he had given up magic, or why, after that school show or after what I had said to him, the magic behind his eyes had died.

He didn't last in the shoe shop. They threw him out. He got another job delivering onions in his beat-up car, but then he lost that when the police caught him for drink driving. He started cleaning houses for a living. Then he got another job.

At the time I didn't know that he was going through all these jobs in different places and that he had given up magic. It was only when I was sixteen years old and in my last year at school that Mum told me that Dad, in those last few months he spent with us, had begun training as an orderly in a mental hospital. He had trained and worked for three or four months and one day, as Mum told it, he didn't return from work. When my mum went to the hospital to find him, they said he had been taken ill himself and had volunteered to stay there as a patient and had been admitted.

Sonia and I were not told about any of this. We found out years later that Mum visited him regularly when we were at school and pretended that he was on tour all that time. And then one day they told her that he had run away. The police were called but they didn't find him. Mum kept all this very quiet from us. She just worked and looked after us and didn't let us see her cry. She secretly phoned his family in India but they didn't reply. Finally the letter from India came. He was there and he was going to find his way in the world, it said. I knew she missed him terribly.

His family didn't like her because he had run away with her and come to England to do magic and they didn't think that doing magic as a profession was good enough, she said.

"Of course it's good enough, it's on TV and some of those magicians are famous all round the world and they are millionaires," I said.

"Your father did an old-fashioned kind of magic. The magicians nowadays use hidden cameras and holograms and all sorts of mind-bending tricks. Your father could never keep up with that. He knew it."

And when she said that I remember what I said to him the night Saffy died.

"You are a useless magician," I said.

That sentence had haunted me from the moment I said it. It was untrue, unjust and... and cruel.

The years passed and every day, several times a day, I would imagine him in strange rooms with strange people. Sometimes with another woman, sometimes with other children. And I desperately wanted to know if he ever thought about us. Did he hate me? All of us? I told myself that even if he did, I would find him one day and find out. I could have a job and could be earning some money and could travel in India, which is where I thought he was. If he was still alive.

Only last year I finished school and came to university in Cambridge. And yesterday, yes, just yesterday my friends and I were going home after an afternoon party when we spotted a circus on Midsummer Common. The three friends I was with decided they wanted to see what this Indian circus was like. They persuaded me to go and I went. It would be a laugh.

And there he was. The ringmaster announced him. He was now calling himself Aflatoon The Magic Goon. He came on and bowed and began his first trick to the music of the band, making a tray of teacups rise from the table on its own. He said, "begi-begi and jill-jillie" and my heart raced and tears came to my eyes. It was Dad.

I waited until the end. I didn't tell my friends what I was doing but I went round the back of the Big Top to the small tents where he was taking his make-up off.

He shut his eyes as I walked into the tent.

"Oh, God," he said.

"Why didn't you come home?" I asked.

"Is your mother there?" he asked.

"Of course," I said.

"And she never..."

"No. She never married again or found anyone else."

"I was afraid," he said.

"Of us?"

"No. Of having run away," he said and he got off the stool and hugged me and cried on my shoulder. He said he desperately wanted to come back. Magic.

# Cut Me, and I Bleed Khaki

## TERENCE BLACKER

*Cagny, France, July 1944*

You can kill almost anything when you are at war but you can't kill a ghost.

Ghosts belong in old country houses with creaky floorboards and hidden stairways. They are for times when fear is something freakish and unusual. At a moment like this, when it is in the air that you breathe night and day, they are the very last thing you would expect to see. Ghosts have no place when the living are trying to kill one another.

And yet I saw one. The ghost was there in front of me, standing, wide-eyed, in a thicket at the end of a lane. We stared at each other, him and me, for ten seconds, twenty, more. I felt my hand, clammy with sweat on the trigger of my machine-gun. Then, as he gazed into my eyes, I knew, I understood. I relaxed.

I haven't told the lads about the ghost, and I probably never will, even if I return home alive after this lark.

In the six weeks of action since we landed on that beach in Normandy, I've discovered that soldiers can talk about missing home and their girlfriends, they can be rude about the officers or make jokes about the enemy, but there is one thing that is never mentioned and that is fear.

Fear makes you weak and, in war, weakness kills.

So I shall write it down. As I sit, leaning against an apple tree, warmed by the evening sun, I gaze at the notebook my mother gave me for my fourteenth birthday, its black leather cover bent and stained by the sweat of war.

Most of the boys are catching up on some shut-eye under a hedge nearby. Today is the first time for almost a week that we have been able to spend time out of our tanks and rest. We've certainly found ourselves a cushy billet in this little orchard. No tanks have churned up the grass and crushed the trees, no shells have pitted the ground. It is the end of a still summer's day, a blackbird is singing in a tree and the sun is high in the sky. If it were not for the rumble of artillery on the horizon, the scene might almost be normal.

But some of us, even after two solid days of fighting, are unable to close our eyes. In a far corner, I can see our squadron leader Major Bathurst as he writes to the mothers, fathers and wives of those who have died over the past week. One or two of the men have found themselves a quiet tree and are writing home.

Under a cherry tree near to where I am sitting, Sergeant "Mosh" McMullen sits gazing across the fields as if, at any moment, enemy tanks might appear. He catches me looking at him and allows a rare smile to flicker across his face.

Yesterday, after the business with the Tiger, it was the sergeant who took me aside.

"Today, Skinny," he said, "you became a man. You became a soldier."

I smiled, shrugged modestly, like a man, like a soldier, should. "Thanks, Sarge," I said.

Maybe he was right. But if he was, how is it that right now I feel like a child?

☆☆☆☆☆

At times likes this, I think of my father, Sergeant Danvers. How would he be now, resting after battle? In my mind, I can see him, small, broad-shouldered, his eyes narrowed against the evening sun.

Little soldier. For as long as could remember, that was what he called me. Back from exercises or from drill at the barracks, he would stride into the bungalow where we lived, give my mum a kiss, then turn his attention to me.

In the early days, we would play the same game every day.

When I heard him open the front door, I would

hide under the kitchen table. He would come in, chat away, until I made a noise.

"Sssh!" he would say suddenly. "Did you hear something, Mrs Danvers? I'm sure I heard a noise."

Beneath the table, I would move again, giggle.

"I did. It's a burglar!" And he would be down upon me, grabbing me, tickling me, rolling across the floor, hugging me with mock ferocity. "Here he is! I've got him! He's a strong little thing, Mrs Danvers. He's a little soldier."

Then, after a minute or so, it would suddenly be over. "There you go, little soldier."

He would stand up, ruffle my hair, and slip back into the mysterious world of grown-ups, hardly speaking to me until it was time for me to go to bed when, a glass of whisky in his hand, he would wink at me. "Night, son."

On my fifth birthday, my father gave me a pair of boxing-gloves. He slipped them on to my hands, tightened the laces on my wrist and sat forwards in the kitchen chair. "Have a go then, son. Give me an old straight left to the face." I can see his wide smile now as he presented me with his face, my target.

I drew my left arm back and punched him, fast and strong, on the point of his nose. To my horror, a terrible sound, a sort of wet muffled crack, could be heard. My father put his hands to his lower face.

When he lowered them, blood was trickling from both nostrils, down over his upper lip, reddening his teeth.

"You little devil, you." He stood up, walked to the sink and dabbed at his nose with a cloth.

"Jim." My mother stood at the door, looking worried. "Jim, don't get angry. It wasn't his fault."

"Hold your tongue, woman." He sat back down on the chair in front of me. His nose was red and swollen.

At that time, I was not afraid of my father. I respected him. He was a soldier in the best tank regiment in the army, a sergeant. He was my dad. Sometimes he shouted at my mum but he was not really a fearsome figure, then.

So it was only because I was upset that I had hurt my dad that made tears well up in my eyes.

"Oh no, boy." A look of annoyance now clouded my father's face. "Don't go and spoil it. You landed a good punch on me." He put his face close to mine so that I could see a thin trace of blood emerging from one of his nostrils. "Enjoy it, little soldier. Enjoy it while you can."

He untied the gloves, pulled them off my hands and returned them to a drawer. I never saw them again.

We moved around. Catterick, Aldershot, Tidworth, Lisburn. As an army kid, you get used to being on your own, to knowing that friendship is something which lasts one or two years at the most.

And my father, somehow, became less Dad and more Sergeant Danvers with every year. I missed the smell of whisky on his breath when he kissed me goodnight. Sometimes it felt as if the last time I had touched him had been when I had landed that punch on his nose on my fifth birthday.

He would go away for weeks on exercises, returning grim-faced and silent, laughing only when I asked where he had been. "Can't tell you that boy," he would say. "Can't risk national security because a snot-nosed ten-year-old is too curious for his own good."

"He was only being interested," my mother would murmur.

And my father would look at her with a cold glance that suggested it was a waste of his precious energy even to answer her. We were background on those occasions. Beside the great matter of the war that was approaching, the everyday things of my life − school, sport, teachers − were trivial.

"We'll be fighting for freedom. Think of that, boy. The future of Europe is in our hands."

Once, a few months before the war began, I asked him whether he was ever afraid. He looked at me with disappointment, almost disgust.

"You're frit, aren't you, boy. Frit that Jerry is going to take you away from your mummy."

I shook my head.

"The army would make a man of you. Would you like that?"

I nodded, not knowing quite what to say.

"I doubt it. I very much doubt it."

One night, my father returned late from the sergeants' mess. He must have been drinking but his voice sounded different, less angry than usual. It was excited, almost boyish. "Mobilization." He spoke as if the word which would take soldiers to war were the most beautiful in the English language. "At last, we're seeing action."

Between sobs, my mother said something about being afraid, about feeling lonely without him.

"Don't talk soft, woman. You'll only make it worse for yourself. You'll have the kid for company."

My mother continued crying.

He never spoke to me about leaving – war, I suppose, was not something children were meant to understand – but three weeks later, he left for France. I remember seeing him rumbling out of the barracks, his head poking out of the turret of a Matilda One tank. I called out to him as he roared past but he stared ahead of him, eyes squinting in the bright sunlight. I never saw him again.

They called it the phoney war, those first few months when the British Expeditionary Force was in

France but never engaging with the enemy, but they felt pretty real to my mother and me.

Now and then, we would get a postcard. My mother would read them over and over again to me, but the words in them – Keeping our spirits up… feeling a little the worse for wear after exercises… last night we raised a glass to the folks at home – sounded like somebody else's.

Among the army wives, there were rumours of where the regiment was based in France but, because no one was meant to know about things, the news was whispered guiltily as if German spies were earwigging on every corner of the married quarters.

It was a quiet time, and one that I secretly enjoyed, but soon the newspapers were full of news from the front. The phoney war was over and the real one had begun.

On the afternoon of 5th June 1940, I opened the front door after school, took one glance at the scene in the kitchen and knew what had happened. My mother sat at the kitchen table, holding her head in her hands as if in prayer. Standing behind her, an arm resting on her shoulder, was our neighbour Mrs Bullen.

"Hullo, Steve," she said in a soft voice.

My mother looked up and said, in a strangely polite voice, almost as if she was talking to an interviewer on the wireless, "Stephen, your father is missing in action.

The War Office have sent us a telegram."

I must have looked confused because Mrs Bullen began to explain, "That means—"

"He knows what it means." Mum spoke as if there were no life left in her, either. "He's an army kid."

I moved across the kitchen and put my arm awkwardly around her shoulder. She leant away from me. For some inexplicable reason, I felt that she was blaming me for everything that had happened.

Soon, around the married quarters at our barracks, it wasn't unusual to have lost a dad. During that spring, the time of Dunkirk, hardly a week went by without another boy or girl in my class getting the bad news. Usually, the first we would know about it would be an empty desk in the classroom. Then, when they returned, nobody would say anything about it although everyone would know. It was like being the member of a club that no one wanted to belong to.

Time heals, they say – but they're wrong. It just makes the pain different, turns it into a dull, ever-present ache of loneliness. The war went on. Sometimes people would talk about the "miracle of Dunkirk", of how thousands of British soldiers were rescued from the beach in northern France by a fleet of little boats that crossed the Channel, but for me there was no miracle. My father was gone. It was only when he was no longer there that I began to realize how important he was to me.

I knew I was supposed to be grown-up – I turned 14 in 1942 and was tall for my age – but I felt as if my father had gone before I had had time to talk to him.

"The army's my family," he used to say. "If you cut me, I'd bleed khaki."

I began to wonder about that. What was so wrong with his real family that it had to take second place to the army?

I had always thought that there would come a day when I could look him in the eye and prove to him that he could be proud of me. Now that day would never come.

My mother was braver than me. She found a job in an armaments factory. She went out with her friends. When a boy at school mentioned that he had seen her in the passenger seat of a jeep driven by an airman from a nearby American base, I realized that she didn't need me at home any more.

And I knew what I had to do.

One dark morning in January 1943, I let myself out of the house before my mother had awoken. Over my shoulder was an old kit bag that I had found in the cupboard under the stairs and had filled with a few clothes. I walked down the road and took the bus into town. I was going to war.

Without anyone knowing it, my school had

helped me become a soldier. There had been a poster in the corridor, meant for older boys, which had the address of the recruiting office of the 23rd Hussars. Maps in Geography had shown me how to get to my destination. The pens in Art had helped me change one small detail on my birth certificate. The year in which I was born changed from 1928 to 1926.

The sergeant behind the desk, a small man with a bent, boxer's nose, glanced at my papers, then up at me. For a moment, he seemed to be considering whether to ask me a few questions but then he thought better of it. It wasn't difficult to join the war effort at that time. I was a soldier at last.

Six months into my training, I knew that I was in the best regiment in the British army. The 23rd Hussars had been set up in 1941 which meant that we didn't have the history, the tradition, the old comrades of other regiments. No one had stories about the way army life had been in the old days because almost all of the men had been civilians until they joined up.

In B Squadron, my outfit, we had a cobbler, a vet, an accountant and all number of factory or farm workers. Some of the men were in their late thirties and had never thought they would fight. A few were in their teens, although none of them was as young as I was.

Sometimes on exercises we would meet blokes

from other regiments. They would be full of boasts and stories about their outfit. Those of us in the 23rd may not have had the airs and graces of those in flashier regiments but we had spirit and some of the best, bravest lads you could ever hope to meet.

The training was hard. There were moments – soaked to the skin in a funk-hole on the Yorkshire moors, hungry and freezing cold in the darkness of the hull of my tank – when I cursed myself for walking away from the comfort of my home that early morning.

As for Mum, I tried not to think of her but wrote a single card in May 1944 when all the talk was of a big push into Europe. I told her I was fine, that I was serving my country and that she could be proud of me.

Two weeks later we rumbled out of the barracks and headed for the south coast. It was time to go to war.

In the hull of the Sherman tank, you are in your own world, dark and sealed up. Inside it reeks of grease and human sweat. In summer, you bake; in winter, the cold reaches into the marrow of your bones. The only people who truly exist for you are the members of your crew.

Major Bathurst, squadron.

Sergeant Mosh McMullen, wireless operator.

Corporal Billy Sims, corporal gunner.

Trooper Johnny "Titch" Garrett, driver.

And then there was me – no longer "the kid" but Trooper Steve "Skinny" Danvers, co-driver, hull machine-gunner, tea-maker.

Beyond that darkness, different kinds of hell can be breaking loose but, to stay sane, you don't think about the horrors of that world outside. You drive, you fire your 75mm. You don't think of the death or injury that, at any moment, could be hurtling towards you.

For three weeks, we were part of a huge traffic-jam of tanks, half-tracks, self-propelled artillery, scout cars and ambulances, hemmed in by the presence of enemy troops some six miles from the Normandy beach where we landed.

One day historians will tell the story of how, on 26th June 1944, the 11th Armoured Division, including the 23rd Hussars, played their part in the battle for Normandy. The truth is, I remember little and sometimes what I do recall I wish I could forget.

Before dawn, the sky behind was a flickering red inferno of artillery as the 600 guns of the Second Army opened up from behind the lines to "soften up" the enemy who were ahead of us. As we waited in our tanks, it was the first time for most of us that we heard the rushing hiss of shells as they flew over our heads, the echoing thud as they exploded two miles away.

Soon after first light, the infantry who were to

lead the attack, the 15th Scottish infantry, rose to their feet and marched into the battle from which most of them would never return.

Then, with a roar of engines, it was our turn. Even before a shot had been fired at us, we realized that this was going to be different from any exercise back home. We were used to moors and plains. Here the countryside consisted of small fields surrounded by steep banks that our tanks climbed, rocking back almost to a perpendicular position before crashing downwards on the other side.

At home, there had been mud. Here, a fine grey dust enveloped every vehicle, clogging the eyes, choking the lungs.

There was no time for fear. Even when we first engaged with the Germans' huge Tiger and Panther tanks, our only thought was for the next action: advance, attack, divert, fire, survive.

Battle changes a person for ever. There were tragedies during the next few days, acts of heroism and comradeship which only someone who has fought could truly understand. Yet, when we were withdrawn and had time to gather around the graves of dead friends – B Squadron had been badly knocked about while trying to take a hill called Point 112 – each of us had only one thought. We have taken what they could throw us. We have come through. There was no excitement about this, no bragging, but a sort of hard, dead-eyed confidence. We weren't ex-civilians, kids or pensioners, the odds-and-sods brigade. We were soldiers.

My father was with me all of this time. Even when the artillery was thundering, when we were in the thick of it, the presence of Sergeant Danvers was there.

He was proud of me. I sensed that, too. And he was going to protect me from harm.

I have never been superstitious but I took it as a sign that, when we were joined by reinforcements from the 24th Lancers, one of them – a Trooper Terry Hagman – turned out to have known him back in 1940.

We were in slit-trench in the shade of a tank when Terry seemed to pick up my surname for the first time.

"Danvers?" He looked me hard in the eye. There was something sour and battle-weary about the man that I didn't quite trust. "You any relation to Sergeant Jim Danvers?"

"He was my father," I said.

"Knew him in France." Hagman drew on his cigarette and gazed into the distance.

"He died there."

"I heard."

Mosh McMullen must have noticed that this mattered to me, that I needed to know more.

"Skinny wants to know how his dad died."

"Yeah?" Hagman looked at his cigarette, enjoying the moment of drama. "He was strafed – machine-gunned – from the air," he said casually. "He died as he lived."

I glanced at him and for a moment he seemed to be considering whether to tell me more about the way Sergeant Jim Danvers met his end, but I had heard enough.

"That's good." I said. "It's all I wanted to know."

"You're right," said Trooper Hagman. "That's all you want to know." And the conversation moved on.

† † † † †

Those first few days of battle had changed us more than months or years of training ever could. For the first time, we felt as if we were part of a great force, that we could win. We believed that, with the artillery behind us and the RAF boys supporting us from the air, we could do the job. It was not going to be pleasant. Not all of us would see it through. But it would be done.

There were other things we had discovered. The German tanks, Tigers and Panthers, were bigger than ours, their armour was thicker and their guns had a longer range. Our Shermans were what we called "quick brewers" – more than any other tanks, they burst into flames within moments of being hit. The greatest danger facing those of us inside was being burnt alive.

But now that we were in the thick of it, we didn't talk about the danger or the glory, death or victory. We simply concentrated on the next task ahead – a bridgehead to hold, a hill to defend, a ridge to be taken. Above all, we didn't think too much. Thinking was for later.

There was to be a big push – some of the lads had heard that it was going to be the biggest armoured advance of the war. 11th Armoured Division was to be in the group leading the attack across the cornfields south of Caen.

It was not a simple task. First of all, we had to cross a river at dead of night and with no radio contact in order to form up for battle on the far side. Then there was another little problem. The first thing that we would reach as we advanced would be an enemy minefield. Three lanes had been made through the mines and we were to follow those lanes. Only once we were through could we fan out and begin our advance in earnest. Our mission was to take a ridge seven miles into enemy territory.

We made the crossing and, at dawn on 18th July, a square mile of armoured vehicles sat, glinting on the sun, waiting for its moment. From behind us, we heard the distant hum of aircraft. Bomber Command was on its way to drop a heavy load on enemy positions four miles ahead of us. As great black Lancaster bombers, escorted by Spitfires, droned over our heads, we stood on our tanks and cheered. It was the moment of truth at last.

Before our eyes, the quiet landscape erupted under the bombardment – first of the Lancasters, then the medium bombers and finally under shellfire for artillery.

Then it was our turn. Beside me, Titch started up the engine, crews settled into their turrets. We moved forwards, slowly at first as we made our way in single file over the minefield, then on at full tilt.

It was like driving over another planet. Everything living seemed to have been destroyed and was still smoking after attack from the air – cornfields, villages, churches, woods.

After a couple of miles, we reached the first of the German troops. Those that had survived the bombing and shelling were in no fit state to fight. Some were grey-faced zombies, staggering past us, too dazed to be afraid. Others were still in their dug-outs but were shaking and shuddering from the shock of the bombardment.

"Poor beggars," I called out to Titch as we thundered past.

He laughed as if I had made some kind of joke. "They don't know what hit them," he said.

We crossed one railway, then two. We were still a couple of miles from the ridge we were meant to be taking but suddenly we came under enemy fire. It was when we emerged from a small village that the major saw something that made him halt our progress.

Some 500 yards ahead of us, on an open plain, a squadron of tanks stood motionless. They were completely exposed to enemy fire, or at least they would have been were it not for the fact that the roar of anti-tank guns from the ridge ahead had fallen silent. There was something strange about the stillness of the scene, with the blanket of dust that had settled on the tanks making them look like ancient forgotten monuments in a grey desert.

The tanks were Shermans. Looking through his field-glasses, Major Bathurst told us they belonged to the Fife and Forfar, the regiment that had been leading us into battle. The question was: why had they stopped?

Standing on his tank, the major glanced at his watch. His orders had been to advance at speed but there was something about the sight ahead of us which worried him.

We heard his instructions through the headphones. "Take a closer look at that, will you, Sergeant McMullen?"

The sergeant gave the order to move. "Go easy,

Titch," he said.

Our tank moved away from B Squadron, out of cover and on to the sunlit plain. There was a lull in the battle and, as I gazed towards our destination, the sun was warm on my face.

*Little soldier.*

400 yards. 300. Now, in the shadow of one of the tanks, we saw signs of movement. "Looks like they've been shot up." The sergeant's voice was matter-of-fact. "A couple of tanks have lost their tracks. We could be going through a minefield."

Thanks for the good news, Sarge.

200 yards. 150.

*Be alert, little soldier. The enemy can strike you at any time and from anywhere.*

Something made me look to the right towards where the sun shone bright over a clump of blackened trees on some undulating ground.

Movement near a shell crater between us and the wood. It was a man who seemed to appear out of nowhere. Bare-headed, and so covered in grey dust that it was impossible to see what uniform he was wearing, he walked slowly, with a weaving stagger, towards us.

I levelled my machine gun at him, began to squeeze the trigger but the man kept on walking. I looked around me, to Titch, the sergeant behind me, but their attention was on the tanks ahead of us.

Then I realized that something very strange was happening. The Sherman was advancing, but the man's position in relation to us remained the same. For the first time, I could see his eyes in his mud-spattered face. They were an icy blue.

*Did you hear something, Mrs Danvers?* And suddenly I knew, as sure as I know that I am here, writing this to you, that he was back. Here, in the thick of battle, I was with my father again.

At this point, he raised both arms to me, as if imploring me for something, then half-turned towards the group of trees behind him, then back to me.

Something caught my eye in the wood. A glint of metal. There, almost entirely hidden by trees and a small dip in the ground, its gun moving downwards towards us, was a mighty German Tiger, crouching, waiting to attack.

It was the end. *Cut me, and I bleed khaki.*

There was no time to scream into the intercom. I opened fire with the machine gun. The sound echoed across the plain.

The rounds that I fired bounced off the armour of the tank but now all eyes were on it. Calmly, I heard Sergeant McMullen calling for covering fire from the 17 pounder. At the same time, Billy Sims opened up from behind me. There was no time to get inside our hatches. Seconds later, explosions from the wood buffeted our faces as we took cover in the tank like rabbits down a hole.

The bombardment continued for a minute, maybe longer, and for every second of it we expected the explosion from the Tiger that would send us into the next world.

Then, as if at a signal, silence. The sergeant's voice came over the air. "Someone up there likes us," he said.

We opened the hatch. There were several mighty shell craters where the German tank had been – but no Tiger.

"Scarpered behind the hill," said Sergeant McMullen. "We won't be seeing them again."

I remembered the man who had warned me. "There's a survivor to our right, Sarge," I said.

The sergeant halted the tank. "Where was he, son?"

My eyes scanned the ground between where we stood and the wood. Open, dusty plain. There was no one there.

"He… he seems to have gone."

"Battle fever, Skinny?" A day ago, the sergeant's voice would have been angry but there was respect there now. We made our way forwards. An entire squadron of the Fifes had been knocked out. The things I saw over the next few minutes as we called up the ambulance and half-tracks to take away the survivors made me forget our own narrow squeak.

Now though, in the unearthly peace of this orchard, I think about my father and begin to understand how it must have been for him, trying to be a soldier and a father at a time of fear. He returned and, on that battlefield near Caen, he showed me how to be a man. He proved to his little soldier that, before anything else in the world, he was my dad.

It is time to write home to Mother and tell her that I am safe.

# Glorious Fergus

## Andrew Daddo

"It's Clint's."

"Won't he spew if he knows you've nicked it?"

"He won't know, will he?" I said. "Unless someone tells him. And who's going to tell him, Hamish?"

"Not me. I won't tell anyone. Not if you give us a squizz." He was looking up at me the way dogs look at their owners when they want something. Probably food. I pointed the sharp end at him, expecting him to flinch.

He didn't disappoint me, the wuss! He was getting older, but not tougher.

I passed it over, handle first. He took it with bulging eyes and let his fingers wrap around the grip. "It'd be pretty powerful, wouldn't it?" he said.

I nodded.

"Do you reckon we'll get anything?"

"Not if we stand around here yapping about it. Hide it out the front in the agapanthus while I tell Mum we're going, okay? And, Hamish..."

"Yeah?" He was fingering the tip of it.

"Don't get sprung!"

"No worries," he said. Then, "What if I *do* get sprung? What should I do? Why do I have to hide it in the garden, anyway? Why can't you?" He shot the questions at me in a high-pitched whine. I started thinking it might be better to ditch him altogether.

"Because, Hamish, I have to pack the gear and say goodbye. Do you want to come or not?"

He nodded, then took aim at Dad's back tyre.

"Well, if you want to come, you've got to do your bit, okay? You'll be all right; just be smart about it. As in, don't do what you'd normally do – as in anything *stupid* – like taking out Dad's tyre? Just wrap it up in your towel and hide it." He did as I said, then disappeared down the side of the house, running like a roadie with a restrung guitar. He was going to get us busted for sure.

I went inside and stuffed a backpack with snorkels, flippers, wetsuits, towels, drinks and the fruit that didn't have maggoty things or little flies buzzing around.

"See ya, Mum," I yelled, hoping for a "see ya" back without the kiss and questions. I should have hoped harder.

"Where are you off to?" It wasn't even Mum. It was Dad, specs hanging off his nose, paper under the arm and the toilet flushing in the background. Nice.

"Snorkelling." I tried not to sound guilty about it, even though I had nothing to feel guilty about. Yet.

"Excellent. I love snorkelling. Did I ever tell you about the time I snorkelled all the way around North Head?" I started to say yes but he had story deafness. It was getting worse too; we used to be able to interrupt him, but now once he'd started a story he couldn't be stopped.

"I jumped in at Quarantine, which is highly illegal you know – but only if you get caught – and turned left. Pretty scary." He nodded. "Pretty amazing too. You should do it when you're older. There's a spot, just past the ladder that comes down on the true North Head, where it all drops away to nothing. Nothing you can see, anyway, and that's where it gets really cold. Don't know why. It just does. So that'd be the best place to pee in your wetsuit to keep yourself warm. You do pee in your wetsuit, don't you, Fergus?"

I nodded. He smiled. "Dad, I have to go. Hamish's out the front. He's waiting for me."

"Righto, then. Off you go. Remind me to tell you about the—"

"Fergus?" Oh great, now it was Mum. We'd never get out of here. "Where are you going?"

"I just told Dad. Hamish and I are going snorkelling."

"Okay," she said. "And you know the plan, right?"

"Of course. What plan?" As much as I wanted to leave, I knew it was better to leave with the plan, especially when it was Mum's or Dad's.

"We're having dinner at Uncle Ian's place, okay? So you're responsible for getting Hamish there and if you get there before we do, you're in charge."

"No problem! We'll probably snorkel there. It's only one beach around. It should be fun. We might even get something for dinner."

Dad's eyes lit up. "That'd be nice. Are you going to take a line with you? Stuff some bait down your swimmers and all that?" he said. "That's what I used to do. You burley up and watch the fish feed on that for a bit, then you lower a bait down to them once you see the big ones relax with you hovering above them. Fascinating stuff. What bait've you got: pilchards or prawns? It doesn't really matter. It all stinks. I try and tuck it around the side of my sluggoes so there's no smell confusion." Mum and I must have looked at him strangely because he suddenly gave a laugh that was very nervous. "Do you want a hand-line? I'll get one." I shook my head.

He stopped before he had a chance to go. "Hey, here's an idea. Why don't I come with you? That'd be cool. I'll show you how to do it."

"No, that's all right, Dad. I'm sure you've got a million things to do around here. Really." And I leant on the "really" so he'd get the idea.

Dad shrugged as if he didn't so I looked to

Mum for support. "How about you clean out the shed?" she said to him. "You've been promising for ages, honey." Excellent!

"That's right. I have, haven't I?" He smiled at Mum. I breathed a sigh of relief. Mum pulled her head back, surprised, the way a chook does when it's clucking around a yard, and an extra chin rolled into her neck. "Which means it won't matter if it takes a little longer, will it?"

"Huh?"

"No, some promises are more important than others."

"Huh?" Mum's turn.

"I promised Fergus, didn't I, Darl? That I would be a father to you kids, not just a taxi-driver or a provider or a bank for you to dip into, but a real live father. Someone you can look up to, someone you can want to be. And that means doing things *with* you, not just *for* you."

"You're just trying to get out of cleaning up the shed!"

"I am not, Darl. This stuff's important. It's bondage. It's about a man and his boy."

"Bonding," I said. "And Dad, it's fine. We do stacks of stuff together, really. And Hamish's going to be there, too, and you can't really bond with me when I'm bonding with him, can you? That's what you said you wanted me to do, wasn't it? Become better mates with Hammer?" I looked over Dad's shoulder out the window for any sign of Hamish and nearly died. The tip was waving around above Mum's agapanthus. Hamish was obviously hiding among them, shooting at some imagined enemy in the sky.

"Where is Hamish, anyway?" asked Dad, beginning to look around.

I quickly got his attention before he checked out the window and busted him. I wondered what Mum and Dad would say if I told them the truth. "Oh, Hamish? Yeah, he's out the front rolling around in your agapanthus pretending to shoot things in the sky with Clint's spear gun." I was suddenly glad Hamish wasn't strong enough to pull the rubber back and load it.

Wrong!

The spear took off like a rocket, trailing the safety string behind it. There was a *phoont* noise as it was launched. Mum and Dad turned to look but I grabbed them both by the hand and said, "Dad? Mum? If you really love me and trust me and want to bond with me, you'll let me—" *Clank!* The spear landed on the roof. The safety string from the roof to the agapanthus was the smoking gun.

"What the—" Dad and Mum said together.

"Bloody possums," I said.

"Language," said Mum and Dad, together, again. They were really in sync at the moment. "Didn't sound like a possum," snarled Dad. "It sounded bigger. I wonder if those bloody Humpy kids have finally started throwing rocks at our roof after all the ones you've lobbed on theirs?" He gave me the sideways look that always made me feel guilty – even for the things I'd only thought about doing.

Hamish's head popped out of the agapanthus. I almost laughed at the look of horror on his face. His head ducked down again, then came up slowly. He stayed low cradling the spear gun as he pulled the string to get the spear back. It *clunked* across the tiles.

"Definitely a possum," I offered. Mum, Dad and I stared at the ceiling and listened.

"Mmm," went Dad, "maybe."

"You were going to get rid of the possums ages ago," Mum snapped.

"I thought I did," said Dad. "That's if it *is* a possum."

There was silence. I stole another look out the window and Hamish was now standing up, in plain view, tugging at the spear line. Obviously the spear was stuck.

"Want a beer, Dad?" I tried to change the subject.

"It's ten o'clock in the morning, Fergus. I like your action, but no. No, thanks. It's not a great idea to drink before snorkelling."

"You're not still coming, are you?" I said.

"Of course I'm still coming. No question about it."

"What about the shed?" said Mum.

"I'm not taking the shed, Darl. That'd be stupid. Sheds don't snorkel." He gave me one in the ribs while Mum gave him one. And his would have hurt. Mum sucked her teeth, grabbed her bag and asked if anyone had seen her car keys.

The roof clunked again, Dad looked back to the ceiling and I looked out the window at the spear that was now free of the roof and flying straight for Hamish. He ducked, but the muffled cry that came through the window made it sound as if he'd still got nailed.

"It's a possum," said Dad. "Definitely. I'll have to sort that later. Hang about, Ferg. I'll get my gear."

Alone in the living room, I could see Hamish in the agapanthus with tears in his eyes, and rubbing his arm. No blood, no problem. I knocked on the window, got his attention and signalled for him to hide Clint's spear gun. He nodded but did nothing. I shook my head.

"See you, later," said Mum. It was more of a huff than a sentence. Hamish dived into a daisy bush as the front door banged, Dad yelled out to ask where Mum was going, she grunted something about a massage, told me to look after Hamish and left.

Great. How did doing the right thing like saying "goodbye" always turn bad?

I took off, collected Hamish and the spear gun on the way. I legged it like the Prime Minister on a morning walk, but it turned out to be too fast for Hamish. He was stuck between a walk and a run, like a trotter gone wrong.

"What's the hurry?" he puffed.

"My dad thinks he wants to come with us, so I figure if we're gone before he notices, he'll realize he'd rather watch the footy or something like that."

"Right."

"And cover the spear gun with your towel, will you?"

"Right," he said again. He was puffing.

I stopped dead and turned to him. "And what the hell were you doing shooting the stupid thing at the house?"

"I didn't—"

I gave Hamish the look.

"I didn't mean to," he spluttered. "I was just trying to see if I could pull the rubber all the way back to load the gun, and then when I did I knew I had to unload it – and the only way was by pulling the trigger. It flies, eh?"

"Yeah," I said. "Straight at the house!"

"Yeah, well—"

*Honk! Honk! Hooooooooonk!*

We turned around to see Dad's Magna tailing us, headlights flashing, and Dad waving like a kid at an aeroplane window.

Busted!

I suddenly got that feeling somewhere between

the pit of my stomach and my butt and didn't know whether I was going to spew or need new undies first. "Cover the spear gun," I hissed.

"I already did," he hissed back. Hamish looked as if he'd be going for the fresh undies – which made me feel better.

The car pulled up with a squeak of the brakes and Dad leaned over to wind down the passenger window. "Good idea getting a head start, Fergus! Hop in, boys, and I'll drive you to the beach."

"We're all right, Dad. We're nearly there, anyway."

"Well I'm not going to shadow you there like some kind of weirdo, am I? And I am coming with you, so get in." I looked at Hamish, who had the spear gun standing behind him in his towel. "Wouldn't you rather get a ride than walk, Hamish?"

"Yes, Uncle Ridley."

"Then get in, son."

Hamish wasn't really used to not doing what he was told to. He moved towards the car, still trying to hide the spear gun, but it was useless. To get into the Magna he had to pick the gun up and even though Dad missed a lot of things, he wasn't going to miss that. "Bit too much starch in your mum's washing, Hamish?"

"Huh?"

"Your towel's a funny shape, son." Hamish glanced at his towel which was sticking straight out the back door. The look on his face reminded me of the time he'd peed in the back seat of our car on the drive home from Yamba.

Dad gave him the look that asked what it was without actually having to.

"Spear gun," said Hamish, his voice on the wobble. Dad gave me the raised eyebrows as if it was my fault and I shrugged as if I had no idea what he was talking about. He shook his head, I lowered mine.

"Fair dinkum, Fergus." *Here we go*, I thought. *Here comes the spray!* I knew that if I had flogged Clint's spear gun by myself I would have gotten away with it. But the moment I try and do anything for someone else – like take my cousin spear fishing or say goodbye to my parents so I can stay out of trouble – is the moment I get smashed. I braced myself. Dad looked ready to blow. The hairs sticking out of his nose were twitching, the sort of thing that would've made lesser men sneeze. "I have been looking for that stupid thing for ages. That's why I took so long to catch up with you."

"Sorry, I didn't know," I said, not knowing why I said it. When in doubt I knew what to say: "please", "thank you" and "sorry, I didn't know".

"Of course you didn't know! It's not as if I was going to ask you in front of your mother. 'Hey Fergus, where's your brother's spear gun? I reckon we should take it snorkelling?' You know how she feels about spear guns. She hates them, whereas I should be the one who *really* hates them. After all, it's my mother with the scars, not hers."

"Huh?" said Hamish.

"Dad shot his mum with a spear gun when he was a kid."

"Gon? You shot Gon with a *spear gun*?"

"It was an accident."

Silence. Then, "You shot *your mother* with a spear gun?"

"I told you, Hamish, it was an accident. It could have happened to anyone, really. It was just plain bad luck that it happened to me – and to her."

"Geez! I can't believe you shot your own mum!"

"Shut up, Hamish, and get in the car before I..." Hamish pushed the spear gun in my direction, "decide not to drive you," Dad finished.

Hamish cocked an eyebrow at me, but I let it go.

"Anyway," said Dad, "that was a long time ago and I've learnt all about water and refraction and that even though things look like they might be out of the way from on top of the water, they still might be *in* the way once you get under the surface. One day I'll tell you about it. First, I've just got to duck into the service station and pick up some bait."

We drove in silence for a bit after that. Hamish broke it with a whisper. "I didn't know you were supposed to use bait on a spear gun," he said.

"You're not," I said.

"No," chortled Dad, easing the car into the servo and wincing at the sound of the brakes. "Although that's not a bad idea. I need the bait for my hand-line and I was also thinking we could burley up a whole mess of fish, then ping off the big ones with the gun."

"Not bad," said Hamish. "Do you reckon it'd work?"

"Maybe," I said.

"Definitely," said Dad over his shoulder.

He came out of the shop with all sorts of stuff, including a couple of Mars bars that hammered back the memories of another drive in another car. I offered Hamish my towel, but he didn't remember. He might have been too busy forgetting.

There was nowhere to park near the beach so we backtracked almost all the way home. "We would have been better off just walking," said Dad. Hamish and I said nothing.

We walked to the beach in our wetsuits because Dad said it was pointless taking the rest of our stuff. "By the time we get back to where we've left everything some backpacker or shifty itinerant would have knocked it off, anyway. It's better like this."

For us, definitely. For Dad, I wasn't so sure. His wetsuit was ancient: pre-velcro. A nappy bit hung from the back and went up between his legs to the front where it was fastened with two rusty press-studs. Instead of doing it up, he let it hang like a rubber dag off his backside so it didn't rub on his inner thighs. "I hate the chafe," he winced. The footpath was hot enough for me to wish I had my flip-flops. I did think about walking in my flippers, but not for long.

I got Hamish to carry the spear gun because I didn't like the way people looked at me when I had it. Carrying a spear gun was completely different from carrying a fishing rod. People seemed to like fishing rods, the way they seemed to like the people who carry them. "Get any?" I always asked when I saw someone with a fishing rod, before I looked in their bucket just to see if they did. Sometimes people didn't like to show you, but that was usually when their fish were undersized. And then I asked what bait they used and exactly where they caught their fish, as if I was going to have a crack myself. But with spear guns, you couldn't say, "Shoot anything?" It didn't sound good. People looked sideways, like they did on a bus when someone farted and no one could work out who. It was better for Hamish to carry the spear gun. If he wanted to look like some sort of enviro-terrorist, that was his problem. I was still going to use it first.

We got to the beach and Dad said, "Rightio, boys, do us a favour and divvy up the bait. You can stick it where you like, but this is where I put it." He stuffed a handful of frozen prawns into each side of his sluggoes, and organized a hand-line down the front.

"I'm glad he didn't bring a hand-line for us too," said Hamish, and I suddenly worried that he might have jinxed us by saying it and that Dad would pull two more hand-lines out from somewhere else and say, "You're in luck, boys!"

"Why do we have to fill ourselves up with bait if we're not using the hand-line?" I asked. Hamish stopped filling his pockets with prawns.

"You *will* be using the hand-line," said Dad.

"No, I won't."

"Yes, you will."

"No, I won't."

"Yes, you will."

"No, I won't." My voice went up at the end and that was a sure sign I was going to crack.

"How old are you now? Four? Five?"

I went to answer, but he cut me off. "Ferg, you *will* use the hand-line because you will *want* to use the hand-line, not because I *tell* you to use it. Mmm?"

"I don't think so," I said.

"If you don't carry your own bait, you can't use the hand-line. That's the deal."

"Too easy," I said. "Take as much bait as you want, Hamish."

Dad shrugged. I could tell he was disappointed, but

I didn't want my board shorts stinking of bait. Not these boardies, anyway. They were too new to stink.

Hamish loaded up – front pockets and back. What a suck.

There was a lecture, of course, about the spear gun and who was going to use it and how it was going to be used and what the rules were.

"I bet your mum didn't give you a lecture before you shot her, did she?" I was asking for it, but couldn't stop myself. Dad let it go with a closed-eyed-head-shake.

"Anyway," he said, "everyone has to stay behind whoever has the spear gun. And, whoever has the spear gun is not allowed to shoot backwards. And, that's about it. Last one in's a rotten egg. He took off for the water, the nappy part of his wetsuit bouncing on his behind like a platypus tail. I followed, duck footing to the shore break with Hamish behind, yelling, "Wait!"

I copped a spray from Dad as soon as I got to the water for running with the spear gun, which was pretty annoying because he was the one who'd started the rotten egg race, not me. I made a *you stink* face at Hamish, who looked as if he didn't know what I was talking about, so I shook my head and stuffed my face in my goggles before Dad could tell me to spit in them.

The water was pretty clean. Not Heron Island clean,

but not filthy either. I made a note to self to avoid any giant clams, just in case. I held the spear gun in front, like one of those fire torches in a dark cave. I wasn't allowed to pull the rubber back until we were away from the beach, so it was kind of fun to pretend to do something else.

My goggles fogged up before they filled with water – which was a first – so I hit the surface to defog and saw Dad, treading water and baiting his hand-line. He looked over and smiled at me. "How good's this, Ferg?"

I smiled back, wanting to say "pretty good", but I didn't. I just swished water around in my goggles to take the fog out.

"Did you forget to spit in them, mate?"

"No, Dad. I don't do that. Why would I want to gob into my goggles and let my eyeballs swim around in it when the goggles fill up with water? It's off."

"Yes, it is, son. But, apart from washing your goggles with toothpaste before you use them – which is good but it burns your eyes – "gobbing" as you call it is the only way to de-fog." He gave me that all-knowing smile before letting a little gob go into his own goggles and swirling it around. He put them on his face and said through his snorkel, "Njhust nhremembah. Nhew stay ahead, nhokay?" I gave him two thumbs up, spat into my goggles, swirled the gob as Dad had and started swimming for the rocks.

And fishing glory.

Hamish had been given a brand new underwater watch for his birthday. I knew that within fifteen minutes a beep would go off to tell him – and then he'd tell me – that it was his turn with the spear. I kicked harder, hoping to run into something shootable before my time was up.

You couldn't just go pinging anything when you had a spear gun. Like normal fishing there were rules: size limits, bag limits, protected species and protected areas. You couldn't see a lobster in the rocks and shoot it, even though that would've been good, because you can't shoot lobster. That was the law. But you could shoot lots of other stuff, like flathead, which were pretty easy to nail because they just lay on the bottom waiting for other fish to swim by so they could inhale them. Or leatherjacket, or bream, or blackfish or morwong or just about every other fish you could think of. There was one rule I'd heard Dad drum into Clint – "No pinging the pretties. If it looks like it might fit in at the Great Barrier Reef, maybe it does and maybe it's lost, so give it a chance to find its way home. Nobody wants to kill Nemo, right?"

After a bit of grunting I pulled the rubber into the go-groove.

I was ready.

I checked that Dad and Hamish were behind me and switched the safety button to "off". I was definitely "on!" which is probably why I didn't see any fish. I wasn't really surprised. If I was a fish and I saw me swimming through the water with a menacing leer on my face and a spear gun in my hand I reckon I'd sense something was up.

I dove for the bottom, which was further than it looked, and found nothing but sand. There wasn't a lot happening round the rocks, either. A few skanky fish hung around the weed, but there was nothing worth having a ping at. I started getting desperate.

"Fnherg! Fnherghus! Come nhere, hwick!" It was Dad, yelling through his snorkel. I turned and headed for him and Hamish, who were heads down, bums up in a school of yellow tail. Dad had the hand-line out in front of him and it went straight down tight towards the bottom. I wondered why he was using such a big sinker, then realized it couldn't have actually been a sinker because the line was moving out to sea.

"What is it?" I yelled.

"Dunno," said Dad, as he ripped his goggles off his face. "There was a big shadow near the bottom so I seafood-cocktailed the hook – two prawns and a pilchard tail – and lowered it as fast as I could and *bang!* The line just took off. I haven't seen the fish at all, but I reckon it's a kingfish – that, or a tuna. Or a shark. Yeah, maybe it's a shark. It hasn't stopped–" he went under, then resurfaced "–running and I'm nearly out of line. If I put the brakes on him he'll either drown me or snap me off."

"Do you really think it's a shark?" asked Hamish, as he started kicking for the shallows.

"I dunno what else it could be. Not much else runs like that."

"I might get out," he said. "I'm getting cold."

"Me, too!" I said. There was no way I was swimming round with a spear gun if there was a pissed-off shark down there with a hook in its mouth. What if it saw me and the spear gun and got the idea I might be wanting to have a go at it too. I'd be dog meat. "Seeyaslater, Dad!"

"Don't you go anywhere!" he barked and disappeared under water. When he came up, he said, "Fergus, I want you to swim down my fishing line and when you get within range of whatever it is down there, I want you to put a shot into it. That should slow him dow–" He sank again. "And hurry!" He coughed when he surfaced.

"You *are* kidding!" I said. "It's bad enough that I'm up here! There is absolutely *no* chance I'm going down there!"

"Aren't you curious to know what it is? I mean,

if it's not a shark and it's a kingfish, it could be the greatest kingfish in the history of the northern beaches. Don't you want to be part of that?"

"Not if it's a shark. See ya, Dad. Wouldn't want to *be* ya!" I followed Hamish who was now halfway to shore and not looking back. Dad had gone under again so I waited to see whether he'd surface. He did with a roar.

"Fergus! Bring me that bloody spear gun! *Now!*"

"I'm not going down there, Dad," I said. And I meant it. The same as I meant it when I'd said, "I love you, Dad. But if you kiss me again in front of Winona I might have to kill you."

"Geez, son. Help me, please. I'm only doing it for you, anyway. Help me—" He went under. "Help you! Help me, help you!" It was a good line from a bad movie. "Please?"

I thought about it. I could even see the helpless look in his eyes through the water and glass of his goggles. "Help me, help you?" What if we did land it? What if it was a shark? Would that be better than a kingfish? Of course it would. We would have risked our lives to rid the beaches of a killer, a pest, a source of nightmares for every kid who ever saw a clump of seaweed and thought it was something else. And, best of all, we could have been killed doing a community service. We'd get on the front page of the *Manly Daily* for sure. Maybe even the news – maybe there'd be a bravery medal. This'd be great. Maybe. Dad disappeared again, and came back up with a splutter.

"Well, if you won't shoot it, give the gun to me and I'll do it. All you have to do is hang on to the hand-line and try to stay afloat."

That had to be harder than it sounded. Dad kept getting pulled under and he was a much better swimmer than me. And where was the glory in hanging on to a hand-line? A centrepin reel on an ugly stick could be glorious, but not a hand-line.

I thought some more before handing over the spear gun. *Be glorious, Fergus. Be Glorious Fergus.* My head had reverb.

"All right, I'll do it," I said, but it came out quieter than I'd expected.

"What?" spat Dad.

"I said, 'I'll do it!'"

"Excel—" gurgle gurgle, "—lent. Give us the weapon and take the hand-line."

"No, Dad," I said as I swam back to him. I kept my head above water, like Tarzan. "I will take out the monster." Glory will be mine, I wanted to add. It was the sort of thing Russell Crowe would have said.

"Are you sure, son?"

"I'm sure."

It was too deep to see the bottom from the

surface, but I knew it couldn't be too far away. Waves broke here when the Pacific pushed in the big swells, so I just needed more air to get deeper.

"Did you see it? What is it?" said Dad when I came up.

"It's too deep," I puffed. "I'll try again."

"Hurry up! I'm out of line," said Dad.

When my lungs and guts and head were full of air I turned for the bottom.

I kicked hard, holding the spear out in front for courage. My mind was racing. My heart was hammering the walls of my chest.

*Dar dump.*

*Dar dump.*

*Dar dump.*

Jaws!

Be glorious, Fergus. Be Glorious Fergus!

*Dar dump.*

I kicked again, deeper.

*Dar dump.*

*Dar dump.*

*Dar dump.*

Aaaaargggghhh!

I let off the shot.

The spear swam straight and true: straight into the back of the monster that held Dad's hand-line. And I could see how it was taking so much of the line.

It was this massive ball of weed rolling across the sand on the bottom.

I turned for the surface, Dad's line in one hand and the spear gun in the other.

*Dar dump.*

*Dar dump.*

My lungs were burning, my ears screaming. I kicked harder and nearly spewed when the spear's safety line pulled tight. The superball of weed caught it, and given its size I wasn't strong enough to wrench it back.

Above me I could see Dad, treading water with his head down, watching. Below me the weed was quickly disappearing into the depths, dragging me, Clint's spear and Dad's dreams of a monster fish with it. I was stuck in the middle. The line above me slackened. Dad was swimming down for me. When he reached me he dropped the hand-line and wrestled the speargun out of my grip. I headed for air, kicking like a South African in a scrum, and broke the surface just as I thought my lungs were going to burst.

The *dar dumps* disappeared as the salt air flew into me. I rolled onto my back and sucked it up. Beautiful!

I knew Dad'd be spewing. He was down where I'd been, trapped between fame and death. I also knew he wouldn't give a rats about the spear gun or the hand-line. The legend was in the fish.

Go the legend.

He bolted for the surface and reminded me of a breaching whale when he got there.

"I'm sorry, son," he roared as he ripped his goggles off and gulped in air. "I lost it. I lost our big one." He lay on his back as I had, except he was quietly swearing as he recovered. I wondered if I would look like that when I had a son. Probably not. There was no way I'd be wearing a wetsuit with a nappy flap.

After a while he turned to me and said, "It was huge, wasn't it?"

I couldn't lie. "Yep."

"I mean, seriously. That was massive."

"Mmm!"

"Have you ever seen anything like it in your life? I mean ever?"

"Not even at the aquarium," I said.

Dad swore again and looked around. "Where's Hammer?"

In the excitement I'd forgotten all about him, but he was on the beach half hidden by a sandcastle.

"Go and get him, Fergus. We'd better head for your uncle's place. I can't wait to tell Ian. He's not going to believe what's happened here."

I shook my head. "I don't think anyone will."

# Acknowledgements

The publisher would like to thank the copyright holders for permission to reproduce the following copyright material:

"Cut Me, and I Bleed Khaki" copyright © **Terence Blacker** 2006; "Later" copyright © **Simon Cheshire** 2006; "Glorious Fergus" copyright © **Andrew Daddo** 2006; "Begi-Begi and Jill-Jillie" copyright © **Farrukh Dhondy** 2006; "Handheld" copyright © **Daniel Ehrenhaft** 2006. Printed with permission of McIntosh and Otis; "Street Corner Dad" copyright © **Alan Gibbons** 2006; "Twenty Crows" copyright © **Ron Koertge** 2006; "Superdad" copyright © **Francis McCrickard** 2006; "My Dad's a Punk" copyright © **Sean Taylor** 2006; "The Wordwatcher" copyright © **Joseph Wallace** 2006; "Whooosh!" copyright © **Daniel Weitzman** 2006; "The Journey to Ompah" copyright © **Tim Wynne-Jones** 2006